CHRISTOPHER NICHOLS

University. He lives in Dorset with his wife and two children. *The Fattest Man in America* is his first novel.

For more about how the book came to be written, with background to some of the themes and issues it explores, see the interview with Christopher Nicholson on page 248.

The Fattest Man in America

Christopher Nicholson

Constable • London

Constable & Robinson Ltd
3 The Lanchesters
162 Fulham Palace Road
London W6 9ER
www.constablerobinson.com

First published in the UK by Constable,
an imprint of Constable & Robinson Ltd 2005

A copy of the British Library Cataloguing in
Publication Data is available from the British Library

ISBN 1-84529-118-2

Printed and bound in the EU

1 3 5 7 9 10 8 6 4 2

To Kit

1

I guess it's only right and proper if I begin with my name, Mickey. That's what you'd call my business name, my stage name. I was given it by Hiram Cutler, my business manager, my erstwhile business manager I should say. Mickey's the name most folk in Drake know me by. To my family, my flesh and blood, my ma and my sisters, to Martha, I'm Michael.

I've been called a good few other names over the years. The Colossus of Drake, to take but one. The King of Fat, to take another. My body has been described as a monument of fat. That's how people think of me, it's my defining characteristic. I'm not podgy, not tubby, not chubby, not stout or overweight. I'm fat. Extremely and excessively fat. The medical term is obese; I was clinically obese years and years ago.

People try to hide their fat. They're ashamed, so they wear loose-fitting clothes, they breathe in, they cheat on the scale. Even when there's no one else watching, they cheat themselves; they adjust the dial so they'll seem lighter than they are. I've never been like that. I'm not ashamed, I know I'm fat, and I've never tried hiding the fact. There wouldn't be no point. I used to ask folk who'd come to see me, in the early days, how heavy d'you think I am? They were always way off, unless they'd been told in advance. They'd stand frowning, scratching their heads and sizing me up, chins cupped, before guessing: four hundred pound? Five hundred?

Nope, I'd say. No sir. No ma'am.

Six hundred? Six fifty?

Keep going.

It's a commonplace how big numbers cease to mean much. Like the distance from here to the nearest star, excluding the sun. I guess it's maybe the same with someone in a visual sense. When you go off the end of the scale, you go off the end of the scale.

Seven fifty? Okay, eight fifty?

They'd get there in the end. Eight seventy-eight. Yes, sir. Yes, ma'am. Not that it's easy being weighed if you're as heavy as me. An ordinary scale, the kind of scale you might buy from a hardware store in Drake, is no good at all. The reading gives out at two fifty or three hundred pound. You might strike lucky and find one that goes up to four hundred, but no higher than that. Anyway that kind of scale's no good; I mean getting on the little platform for a start, and then trying to read off your weight on the indicator display when your stomach's blocking the view. It's no good at all. The only way I can weigh myself is on an industrial weighing machine, and that's what we had installed here at the Fattest Man. It was a scale designed to measure the weight of grain.

That's weight. It's not the same as fatness, of course. Weight's intangible. Weight exists only on account of gravity, the force identified by Sir Isaac Newton in England, U.K., in the seventeenth century, and to which we are all of us tied, being earthbound. Like soft, invisible glue. Like an elastic band, holding each one of us down. If there was no gravity, if the elastic band was suddenly cut, we'd float up to the stars.

Now mass is something yet again. Technically speaking, I believe mass is defined by the matter in an object as measured by its resistance to change of motion. It's my mass, not my weight, that always impressed folk most. Or, to be more precise, the quantity of flesh that I possess, and the way it sprawls and flows away from me like it's a separate being. I didn't fully understand that at first, how anyone could see it as separate from me, but that's how it was. It was the flesh that fascinated them. Intrigued them, challenged them. Horrified them, sometimes.

One day for instance, it must be about three years ago, this woman in red pumps and red skirt shows up in the Shrine. She's quite old, thirty-five, forty, I don't know, with frizzy brown hair and a bleached complexion and tight lips. She seems slightly nervous, biting her bottom lip. She kneels down, quickly, like she's planned out exactly what she's going to do, and places the fingers of her right hand on the side of my belly. Her pale hand rests on the pale expanse of my belly like it's testing for something. She begins to kind of stroke the flesh, caressing it in a downwards motion. I haven't paid too much attention so far, but now I watch her pretty closely. She carries on for maybe a minute, gentle as anything, stroking the same section of flesh, and murmuring to herself all the while. Her lips are moving, it's like a prayer. Then she leans forward, brushes her lips against the skin she's been stroking, stands up, smooths down her skirt and leaves. That's it. Very brisk and businesslike. But every day for the next few days she returns, choosing a different section of flesh each time. Like she's working in a systematic way over the whole landscape. Not just my belly, but my legs as well, and on one visit she strokes between my toes, all my toes, very slowly, the big toe down to the little toe, like she's playing with each toe.

Martha reckons it was sexual, she reckons I don't understand female sexuality, but most of the time this woman's demeanor wasn't so much sexual or erotic as religious, or at least reverential. That was how I took it, the way her lips would move like a prayer, I took it as a kind of ritual. A piece of flesh worship. That was Hiram's view too. She was worshipping the flesh. And I was largely irrelevant, even if the flesh did happen to belong to me.

The story doesn't end there and I'll say more about it later on, but before then I ought to fill in some background, because I wasn't always so very fat. Sure I was always on the fat side, but when I look back at photographs that show me as a kid, age six, seven, I look pretty ordinary. Not thin, never thin. But not fat fat. Not fat so folk'd turn to stop in the streets to gaze at me. Not fat so I couldn't fit through doorways without jamming. Not fat so my head seemed

4

like a pea balanced on a block of jelly. That's how the *Colorado Weekly* described me.

I know I wasn't so fat for other reasons. Like remembering playing ball in the backyard. And walking to the Blue Falls, without too much difficulty. I was rising ten then. Running? I'm not sure. I don't recall ever running much but maybe I did once, as a kid.

After nine I don't have no photographs of me until I'm eighteen, and by eighteen I'm something else. This wedding photograph, Hilary's wedding, Hilary being my older sister, I'm bulging like the hell in this purply suit and I look like someone's stuffed me with kapok. I look like a moon man. Know those shots of the moon men creaking in their fat suits? That's me at eighteen. Except the moon men bounced, and I couldn't have bounced.

I don't want to give the wrong impression. Even in those days I could move round easily enough, I could walk. I was working at the Ranelagh Grand, and I'd walk there every morning, and walk back here at the end of the shift, past the drugstore, the movie centers on Arlington, the museum, on to Willard, Jackson's, right up the hill. I'd be breathless and wheezing like crazy, stopping to rest every few paces, but I could do it. I could walk on the porch no problem. I could even walk upstairs, without worrying about falling through the floor.

Well, I couldn't do that now. Couldn't begin. Now, now, I look back and I ask myself sometimes, how did it happen? It's come upon me over the years, the flesh, layer on layer, blubber slapped on like wet cement that dries and then is ready for more. Layer on layer on layer. Slap slap slap. How'd it happen? Answer is, I don't rightly know. Search me. Blame my ma's cooking, if you like. Blame the donuts at Jackson's. Blame the inventor of the pizza. Blame the first guy dreamt up waffles and maple syrup. Blame heredity. Blame my metabolism, blame diabetes, that's where the doctors point the finger. Won't do, though. Not as a total explanation.

I'm not blaming anyone. What I feel is, I feel it's like it's been wished upon me. That's all I can say about it. Like ordained. Not like a curse, more a blessing than a curse. Like I've been chosen by God, and I'm not going to start off blaming Him. Because I look at it this way: if it weren't for being fat, I'd never have met Martha. She likes me fat.

I used to feel pretty proud of my fatness. I used to think how there was no one else like me, not in Drake, not in America, maybe not in the whole world. Did it make me proud? Sure, sure, it made me proud. But currently . . . currently I kind of look on it in another light. I mean I don't think that way any longer; fat or otherwise, I just see myself as an ordinary American.

That's part of the reason why, when you asked me to take part in this oral history project, to give an account of my life up to this point in time, I was kind of doubtful at first. Why me? I'm private, I'm an ordinary citizen, I closed down the business a long while ago. If I get requests for interviews, I turn them down. But oral history, I guess that's fine, and I like it being a local project. Just so long as you don't cut the tapes up too much, because I know what happens, how easy it is to misrepresent what someone says: you get out the razor and start cutting here and there, and moving words around, and in the end they're saying something they probably didn't mean to. Creative editing, it's known as. That's a joke. I call it misrepresentation of the facts.

How I see myself now, I see myself as an American, and a patriot, and a businessman. For instance I'm currently working on a business manual based on my life experiences, for the benefit of my fellow countrymen. It's a big subject, a big challenge.

I haven't begun to write yet, I'm still ordering my thoughts in my head, I haven't even got a title, but eventually I may well dictate it to Martha. Or I'll dictate into a tape recorder, like now. Writing as such, with pen and paper, or typewriter, isn't so easy when you're fat as I am.

★

Drake is the town in which I happen to live. It's close on a city. A nearly city. Population forty-one thousand, and good and busy. It has drugstores, supermarkets, hotels, cafeterias, freeways, churches, a museum. It's got all the things that usually make up a city, but it feels more like a town, I guess. That's all I can say. There's a friendliness in the air. Folk get to know each other even if they don't know each other, if you know what I mean; I mean you walk down Arlington and you don't know the names but you know the faces, they're familiar. Just the other day a month or two back, there was a holdup at a liquor store on Willard and a man was shot, owner of the store, name of Mr. Walter Giddins. Early in the evening he was standing by the check-out when a man comes in the store, shoots him in the chest. No reason. It was a very hot steamy evening, like we get round here, but that's no reason. He was a decent man, a law-abiding citizen, a member of the community. While I didn't know Walter Giddins exactly I knew what he looked like; I mean, I must've walked past that liquor store dozens of times, in the days when I could walk. I knew his face. That's what makes the difference between a place being a town and a city, I guess. But I knew something had happened even before I read about it in the *Drake Chronicle*, because I could hear the sirens wailing. That's another thing: living here, on a hill, the sounds travel up. I can see the whole town laid out in front of me. It gives me perspective. It's good.

Furniture's the main industry. Office furniture, domestic furniture. It has no less than three furniture factories. I can see one from the window that faces west, the C-J Works, where I was employed when I was thinner. This time of year, coming into the fall, the sun sets behind the hills on the far side of Drake. High summer it gets further round.

I was not originally from Drake. I was raised in Constant, fifty mile inland of here. There's a railroad connects Drake and Constant, before winding northeast to Fort Worth and south-east to Houston.

Constant's a much quieter place, not dozy or sleepy but quieter than Drake. It's a big traditional center for the pecan nut industry but I'm not going to describe it, it's not relevant and I want to make my account as relevant to your purpose as possible. My ma still lives there, age fifty-four, as does my younger sister Zoe. I have two sisters, Hilary and Zoe. Hilary's age thirty-one, Zoe's twenty-four.

Hilary lives way up in Richmond, California. She's the smartest of us, she got all the highest grades at school. She's married to a guy works at the University of California, wears little flinty glinty gold spectacles. He's a dinosaur hunter. No, he is, I'm not kidding. He's an expert on the dinosaurs. He's always coming down to Arizona looking for dinosaur fossils.

All of us is outsize. I guess Zoe would be two fifty pound and Hilary a little less. She's a stripling, relatively. My ma's about three hundred and fifty. She's diabetic, like me; diabetes mellitus. It's type two diabetes, it often affects obese people. Then I've got uncles, aunts, they're none of them slim. My Uncle Bobby must be close on three hundred and fifty. Being fat is something my family's gone in for, we've specialized, hereditarily speaking, you might say.

My pa was fat, too. He passed on six years ago, just before I started to swell like a toad—that's another of those pleasant things written about me—and was laid to rest in Rough Creek Cemetery. I didn't have no suit to wear, I'd got too fat for the one I wore at Hilary's wedding, and I was going to wear a spare suit of Uncle Vince's but he forgot to bring it down from Wilmington. So I had to wear my pa's suit, the suit he used to wear to the Baptists. That was kind of creepy, wearing Pa's one and only suit when he should've been wearing it. Sure it would've been a waste of the suit, but I thought he maybe should've been buried in it.

Tell the truth, that suit was too tight for me even then and I was pretty scared it was going to split, particularly when I was one of those bearing his coffin. There was me and Uncle Bobby and Uncle Vince, and the coffin was real heavy. It'd been raining like crazy and Uncle Bobby was grunting with the weight, and I kept on thinking when we came to lower the coffin the suit'd burst open. It didn't, though, for the reason that Uncle Bobby lost his grip and the coffin went down with a crack like it was going to split instead. Uncle Bobby's got an alcohol problem. He's been to rehab clinics and places to dry out but it never lasts long, that's why his marriage to my Aunt Nancy ended in divorce. Recently he got himself married again to a native Indian. He lives in Fort Worth and currently he's selling arms, he's a firearm salesman. He sold me a handgun last time I saw him, a Beretta. It was more than a year ago. I didn't really want to buy it, but since the shooting of Walter Giddins I've begun to think maybe a gun isn't such a bad idea after all.

Pa worked as a carpenter, and my childhood was full of the smell of sawdust and the sounds of sawing and hammering. He made beautiful furniture, chairs, tables, each one designed differently by himself. Nothing like the mass-produced goods turned out by the C-J Works here in Drake, nothing at all. Each one was unique. He'd decorate them with carvings of birds, fish, snakes, reeds. I guess he got his inspiration from what he saw when he was fishing up in Lake Constant, about five mile east of the town. It's a big big lake with plenty of rocky coves and creeks and the mudflats where the mouths of the creeks've silted up and you get birds on the mudflats like ibises and things. There are white-tailed deer in the trees, and raccoons and squirrels and suchlike. My pa didn't go fishing much, didn't have the time I guess, but when he went he caught crappies, or big bass, that kind of fish, if he was lucky, but he never seemed to mind too much if he never caught anything. I reckon he went mainly for the peace and quiet, watching the ripples on the water, being in touch with nature. He was that kind of a man. I went with him sometimes, but he never talked much. Constant's a dark lake, a dark body of water, and he liked watching the reflections on the surface, clouds drifting slowly, pale and dark, meeting other clouds, merging, breaking up, like the lake was one huge alternative sky that faced the real sky, and beneath this other sky the fish moving unseen in the darkness. It's kind of hard to describe but it was like we were on the edge of several different worlds and none of them quite real, more like a dream than real. I used to play a game in my imagination where I tilted everything so the lake was rising before me in a steep slope and I was at danger of falling over backwards.

I had my own rod and I fished, too, or tried to fish. I

liked keeping my finger on the line, waiting for the tug of a fish nosing at the bait. If I got bored, as did happen, I'd wander off and skip stones, or take a swim, or look for interesting pieces of wood along the shoreline. The shoreline's quite heavily wooded in places and you get trees that grow right on the edge, and over time floods wash away the ground about their roots and they crash into the lake. Then they seem to bump around in the depths for a few years before surfacing again and getting washed back to the shore, with all their bark washed off and the wood smooth and polished, like bare bones, or deer horns. I loved the smoothness: like the lake was some great carpenter, turning objects out of its own imagination.

I guess I derived those feelings from Pa, because when he'd finished making something like a chair he used to talk about it like it was alive, and stroke the wood. I have a chair made by him here in this house, in my bedroom, an armadillo carved on the back. It's a beautiful object, it's art. I couldn't ever sit on it, of course, it's too small and wouldn't begin to take my weight, but I like looking at it and thinking how he fashioned the wood so beautifully. I like thinking how he carved the armadillo. He had plenty of talent, my pa and he loved wood, he loved different types of wood. If you'd blindfolded him he'd've been able to say what type of tree a piece of wood came from, just by assessing its weight and running his fingers along the grain of the wood.

One thing Pa didn't have, and that is business acumen. He had not one iota. I don't think he even liked selling

12

the things he'd made; he was too much in love with them, I reckon. As for marketing, proper marketing, he wouldn't even've understood what was meant by the term. I'm not criticizing, as I say, he was an artist, but the result was we never had much money. We weren't poor, we always had food on the table when we were hungry, but the house wasn't so very big and the cars we had were always breaking down in out-of-the-way places, and I always hated that. It was hard enough us fitting in a car anyway, more often than not we'd have to rattle along in the truck Pa used to collect wood from the woodyard, and then it'd break down on some highway. He'd whip the hood up saying it was nothing much, but an hour later we'd still be there with his head stuck in the engine. What I hated was the thought of everyone passing by laughing at our misfortune. I guess they maybe weren't laughing at all, but I imagined they were. Either laughing at us breaking down or at us all being so fat. I've always done my best in life not to laugh at the supposed misfortunes of other folk.

I hated riding in the truck at all. If I was put in the open part at the back I'd lie down not wanting to be recognized by folk we knew. Kids from school, that's who I feared. At school I was teased and taunted a lot, as you'd kind of expect. Fat people are easy targets. I was called the Earthquake, that was one of the nicer names. Hi, Earthquake. Jumbo, Flatfoot, Blubber. It's a cross you have to bear, being fat. The unholy cross of obesity. I always kept silent, as if I didn't hear, but silence isn't as powerful a weapon as some people try to make out. The wounds still go in. You get raw.

My sisters and I were given a good decent education, and taught how to behave respectful. We attended church school, not every week but every month, where we were taught about the Ten Commandments and the Four Gospels, and inculcated with the right values, by which I mean hard work, clean living, and a faith in Providence. We were Baptists. We used to go to a Baptist church off of Clarksville and it was a fine building with this huge baptism tank I was baptized in, like a shallow swimming pool, with blue walls, and steps to get into it. An immersion chamber. I still recall, when I was getting into this swimming pool to be baptized, I recall the hand of the minister pressing down real hard on my head, pressing me under the water, because it was total immersion with the Baptists. If you weren't totally immersed it didn't work; the devil sat on the bit that kept dry. The minister was called the Reverend Candy and he was some preacher, it was scary. He was a little tubby guy in a dark suit but he used to hold us in the palm of his hand. He was like the conductor of an orchestra. He never used notes, he seemed to know great hunks of the Bible off by heart. His favorite text I recall was this. It was this . . . It was from St. Paul, he was very keen on Paul. I reckon he was even keener on Paul than Jesus. Tell the truth I reckon he thought he was Paul himself, reincarnated.

Wait a minute, I want to get this right. I'll get a Bible. This was it, this was it. From Saint Paul's First Letter

14

to the Corinthians. This isn't the text he'd've used, it's a Gideon, but you'll get the idea. It's chapter fifteen, verse fifty to fifty-two:

> Now this I say, brethren, that flesh and blood cannot inherit the kingdom of God; neither doth corruption inherit corruption. Behold, I shew you a mystery; we shall not all sleep, but we shall be changed, in a moment, in the twinkling of an eye, at the last trump: for the trumpet shall sound, and the dead shall be raised incorruptible, and we shall be changed. For this corruptible must put on incorruption, and this mortal must put on immortality.

That was his favorite text, the Reverend Candy. What he used to do, he'd read it through at normal speed then very slow, then he'd take the text letter by letter, phrase by phrase. "Flesh," he'd say. "Flesh. What is flesh? What happens to flesh? It decays, it perishes, it corrupts, it rots. It does not endure. Whereas the kingdom of God does not perish, it does not corrupt or rot, it endures forever. That's what the Evangelist is telling you. Flesh and blood will not endure, and nothing that does not endure will be acceptable in the kingdom of God. Nothing that is of this earth, such as our possessions, our houses, our clothes, none of these is acceptable in the kingdom of the Lord." He'd go on like this about flesh and blood for about five or ten minutes, then he'd move on to the word "changed." "Changed. Changed." He'd repeat the word several times, saying it slightly differently, like it was a strange object he was holding up to the light and examining from different angles. Then he'd say: "What does it mean to be changed? How shall we be changed? What is the significance of that change?" Then when he'd finished with "changed" he'd get on to "the twinkling of an eye" and so on, right through the passage. It was the same with all his preaching, he'd lay the whole thing out word for word. It was impressive stuff.

The point of this text was that the world'd end anytime, any second, without warning, and whatever was happening at that moment the graves'd open and all those who died with God in their hearts would fly out of their tombs toward Heaven. Those who were still alive, if they had God in their hearts, they'd go too, in the twinkling of an eye. I mean the way he explained "the twinkling of an eye," it was going to happen instantaneously. Not even in a second or a quarter second. It was going to be just like that, like God flicking a switch, with no warning at all. I mean people driving along the freeway or something wouldn't even have time to pull over and stop, they'd just shoot out of their cars. I recall Pa saying that it was a good argument for a convertible, and Ma saying that for all those left behind there was going to be one heck of a big crash, all these driverless cars shooting about.

The thing was about the Reverend Candy, he believed the end of the world was going to happen any moment. Any moment now. He'd got it all worked out from the Bible, the Book of Revelation, we were now in the last days. I can't remember all the details, but at some point there was going to be this big final battle against the forces of anti-Christ and then the world would end. I'm not saying he isn't right, after all when you think of the Soviets. I mean the forces of anti-Christ. I don't know. I mean there're lots of people much smarter than me say he's right so I guess they may be, though I can't help wondering how much they believe it, if they take out life insurance for instance. You'd have to ask them, for your project.

I don't know if this is any use to you. There were tapes made of the preaching you could buy the next week, you could maybe get one for your project, I don't know. He was a fine preacher; still is, I guess.

When I must've been about ten we stopped going to the Baptists. I didn't mind it, but my pa couldn't stomach the whole thing. We didn't fit in. Everyone seemed quite rich and prosperous, they were business folk, and all they seemed to care about more than anything was making the church richer, even though the world was ending on Monday, that was all they seemed to care about. Whereas Pa was a carpenter, like Joseph, Jesus's father. He was a carpenter. And in consequence, not having enough money, was kind of looked down upon by the businessmen, or so he felt. There they'd be after the service in dark huddles discussing the church finances, and Pa wouldn't have anything to say, he couldn't join in. So we tried another church, the Church of the Divine Consciousness. It doesn't exist any longer. This being the Bible Belt there're lots of churches, Pentecostalist, Episcopalian, Presbyterian, Church of whatever you like, they all start up claiming to represent the true faith, the word of the Lord; in fact there's

17

one in Drake called the Church of the Word of the Lord. A few get established and keep going, the rest close down, just like businesses. That's the American way, I guess. This one was the Divine Consciousness and it was a pretty new church but it was mostly empty, it was like a failing business. After a time we stopped going and went fishing instead, least Pa and me did, until he passed on.

What I would say is, we were raised as patriots. Early as you like, I knew about the threat of the Soviets. Cuba's not so far from here, and Dallas . . . when President Kennedy was assassinated in Dallas they were sure as anything the Soviets were responsible. I'm sure they were, too, I mean the Soviets, the Russians. I don't recall the assassination any too clearly, I was too young, but I'm old enough to recall the U.S.A. beating the Russians to the moon, and watching on our black-and-white television that day in nineteen sixty-nine when the Stars and Stripes flew for the first time in the lunar landscape. That was a proud day for us all.

I know you don't want my political views but I'd just like to say, if you'd permit me the space, that as I see it there's the political threat from the Soviets, directed through Nicaragua and Cuba, but also Mexico. Sometimes I ask myself if up in Washington if they fully comprehend the volatility of the Mexican situation. This is America's backyard, and freedom's too valuable to be left to look after itself; if you leave the back door unlocked sooner or later someone's going to steal in and rape your wife or steal your property or whatever, if you don't trouble yourself to lock your doors at night. That's what Uncle Bobby says, in his sales pitch, and I'm inclined to agree with him. It's like Nature abhorring a vacuum. On top of that, there's the economic threat from the Japanese. For example, and I'm not blaming you, I notice this little tape machine is Japanese in origin. That's happening everywhere, the United States is being flooded with cheap Japanese imports, weakening our economy and costing us valuable jobs. Now, while I believe in free trade, I also happen to believe, along with the President, the United States has a duty to protect its position as world leader. If you stop, just stop, and imagine the world without the guiding hand of the United States, it's a frightening thought. Now, I've had my say, and I'll return to my own story.

Upon leaving high school I looked for work, and moved from Constant to Drake. I got employment in the C-J Works on the production line, playing my part. It paid me a wage. I liked it. I was mainly in the packaging department, armed with the staple gun. You mightn't call the work exciting, or stimulating, or interesting, but it had its satisfactions. There's something good about stapling cardboard, in that it allows you space to dream. Like many Americans I've always been a dreamer, I guess, like the first Americans who set sail on the other side of the Atlantic Ocean.

I was treated okay at the C-J Works, but a year down the line I felt like a change, and I tried to get work on the railroad. That was always my ambition as a kid, like any kid I guess, I wanted to be the driver. My grandpa on my ma's side, we used to call him Grandpa Connell, Connell being my ma's family name, he used to tell me about the old steam locomotives and the building of the railroads. I still have the dates kind of printed on my memory: eighteen forty-six, incorporation of the Pennsylvania Railroad; eighteen forty-nine, charter granted for the building of the Missouri Pacific Railroad; eighteen sixty, Missouri Pacific Railroad completed. Eighteen sixty-two, Congress authorizes construction of a transcontinental railroad. Eighteen sixty-four, construction begins of the Union Pacific and the Central Pacific Railroad. Eighteen seventy-two, Santa Fe Railroad completed to the Colorado border. I could go on and on. It kind of caught my imagination, the way Grandpa Connell'd talk about it: the amazing labor that went into the building of the railroads all over America, over the Great Plains, the prairies, through the Rockies . . . he talked about it like an act of heroism, of patriotism. Like this was the grid plan for modern America. And I guess he was right, the railroads of the nineteenth century were what laid the foundations for the United States' trade and prosperity in the twentieth. Before then, what was there? What was there? There was the horse and buggy. Constant, for instance, was just this itsy-bitsy little settlement right on the frontier. There were marauding Indians out on the trails. Trail drovers used to drive their cattle down the main street and there was so much dust folk closed their doors and shut their windows. Times were the town was nearly cut off. But then the railroad came. First train that came through Constant did so on December the first eighteen eighty-five, just under a hundred years back, and there was a regular service up and running to Drake by February eighteen eighty-six, and then the town just took off. Suddenly wasn't nowhere near the frontier, because there wasn't a frontier any longer. And Grandpa Connell made it all seem so exciting, the whiteness of the steam and the black face of the stoker feeding the engine, and the wild scream of the whistle and the crowds waiting on the platforms at the depot. They cheered the first trains he said, they hung out bunting and cheered and had a brass band playing, and I understood that, cheering a train. I always wanted to cheer the trains myself, when I saw them come by. And it was my biggest treat, riding on the railroad, when I was a kid.

Well, that was why I reckoned I'd get myself a job on the railroad. Well, there was no position vacant, or that's what they said when I applied.

So I found employment in the Ranelagh Grand. It was the best hotel in Drake then, the only four-star, still is; the competition's not that great, I guess. The only other hotels worth visiting are the Adelaide, which is three-star, and the Best Western, which has just two. They're not bad, they're good enough, but they've nothing fancy about them, whereas the Ranelagh's got flags and tinted glass and Ancient Grecian pillars. In the forecourt's this fountain with a statue of a Grecian goddess, I don't rightly know which, but I guess it's made of bronze or something like it. She's naked, and holding a flower in each hand, and the

21

water, the shoots of the fountain, you know, come out of each flower and meet making a kind of archway of water. It's a good piece of work. Folk throw money in sometimes thinking it'll bring them good luck, and the manager, Mr. Watson, Chuck Watson, used to collect up the money every so often and distribute it among the staff. And when weddings were held you always got the bride and groom being photographed in front of that fountain, with their favorite music playing in the background. There are plenty of weddings at the Ranelagh Grand, or there used to be anyhow, it's a good place. It's four-star. It has seventy-five rooms, swimming pool, restaurant, coffee shop, ballroom, all air-conditioned, and the carpets are real thick. The foyer's black marble, marble floors and walls. The tables in the restaurant are laid with starched white linen table-cloths, like the best restaurants. The menus are all written out in French.

I was a bellboy at first, then I transferred to work in the kitchens under Mr. Tiplady, the head cook. He's meant to've trained in a real French restaurant somewhere like New York, or that was what he always claimed. He was a good cook. Sweets were his specialty. One he made, I don't know what it was in French but he called it a hot marlin. It was delicious. It was a banana lightly fried in unsalted butter then served in a sauce of sugar and cream and brandy. Even talking about it makes my mouth water. Another of Mr. Tiplady's specialties was rich chocolate soufflé topped with fresh whipped cream; on the menu that went down in French as *"nègre en chemise"* but everyone called it "nigger in a nightshirt." Even the waiters used to say to guests, when showing them the sweet trolley, "that's nigger in a nightshirt, sir." It wasn't meant offensive; guests mostly seemed to appreciate the joke. It raised a few chuckles. Of course they were white: black people didn't seem to come to the Ranelagh Grand that much, I can't say why, and there were no black staff except some of the chambermaids, who were mostly Mexicans and other Hispanics.

As a bellboy I wore a smart uniform, dark green, with cap and gold braid, by order Mr. Saker, and gold buttons up to the neck. My job was to hang about near the front desk, keep a watch for new guests, and carry their bags up to their rooms. I was also responsible for room service, and if the hotel was busy for something like a business convention it could be pretty tiring, but I didn't complain. I enjoyed the work. Reason I transferred to the kitchens was my bellboy uniform got too tight. It was the biggest size available but I couldn't breathe. It got to the point I couldn't do up the buttons, even though in those days, of course, I was much thinner than I was to become.

Clothes are a real problem for someone like me. Manufacturers don't cater for what I call the fat community, there's no profit in it, so you have to get clothes made specially. My ma makes me clothes, and there's a guy down in Drake, a tailor, who's run up things for me in the past. Even then, dressing, the business of dressing . . . I mean, how do you put on a pair of pants? Here's how, I'll tell you. You bend and hold them near your feet and put your

23

feet in the holes and pull them up. Simple. Don't even think about it. I used to do it that way too. Now, with me, my mass, my belly, being what it is, the option's no longer available. My arms aren't long enough to reach near my feet, they can't stretch round my belly, and if I try bending my knees they hit up against my belly too. So most of the time I'll just stretch a towel over me or wear nothing at all, as God intended, or slip on a loose-fitting robe. Like now I'm wearing a dark red robe. It's got a drawstring, but my belly flops out; I can't contain my belly like that. My belly often gets pretty cold. What they call the body's cardiovascular system, you know? The central heating system. It doesn't function so well out on the extremities, and even on hot summer days when I feel real warm inside I can put my hand on the outside of my belly and the flesh'll be cold. That's what folk sometimes used to say when they touched it: "Wow, it's so cold! It's like . . . it's clammy!" I don't know about clammy. Clammy? It's thick, all right. Thick flesh. How thick I couldn't say. It wouldn't keep out a bullet. I see it more like clothing, like an insulation. Maybe cold and clammy where they touch but inside, I tell you, I'm good and warm.

Folk always used to ask about that. What d'ya eat? What d'ya store in that sack down there? I'm not sure I can answer too exactly, a lot's gone down there over the years. The short answer is, until recently I've always eaten same as the rest of the American population, only in larger quantities. Cookies, popcorn, pizza, burgers, steaks, fries, spicy food, chili, Tex-Mex, the whole menu. Burritos.

Vanilla pudding, cheesecake, ice cream. Just what you'd expect. But recently I've been diagnosed as type two diabetic, and that's changed things somewhat. Dr. Coughlan, who works at the St. Theresa of Avila Clinic, has advised me to cut down on fat-rich foods, so I don't eat so much cream as I once did and I'm meant to avoid sugary foods. No candy. No donuts. It's all to do with keeping my glucose levels stable. I'm not observing it too strictly, what's the point? I enjoy eating donuts. My opinion is, if you enjoy something go on doing it, so long as it doesn't do anyone else any harm.

To drink? Well, I drink water, iced tea, coffee, diabetic fruit juices, beers. I don't bother with diabetic beer, I drink Lone Star. Definitely wouldn't touch Mexican beer, though I do sometimes drink tequila. It was Martha introduced me to tequila.

I guess if I kept a record you'd say I ate a lot of food, but if you consider my probable weight I don't reckon it's so unreasonable. I'm possibly five times the average weight of an adult American male. Now, if you divide my food consumption by five, does it still seem so much? I wouldn't say so. That's my opinion. I do eat a lot: it's like stoking a boiler, I guess; it needs fuel, and if there ain't no fuel the fire goes out, simple as that. I reckon I could go on eating and eating without stopping, if I wanted to, most of the day and night. But I don't. I'm not greedy. Looking at the Seven Deadly Sins I may be guilty of several, including Pride, but I plead not guilty to Gluttony. I have never regarded my food consumption as that excessive; not excessively excessive. I don't believe it's the cause of my fatness; that's a general misapprehension.

What is a belly? It's a kind of magic beanbag, that'd be my way of describing it. Hollow and flexible, changing shape, swelling and shrinking according to need, storing and processing, like one of those genies used to come out of the lamp. Soon as food arrives down the chute from the esophagus the stomach zaps out chemicals like pepsin and hydrochloric acid like there's no tomorrow, and at the same time it begins churning away like some industrial butter churn. In the end you've got this smoothy creamy stuff that gets squirted on along the production line. Not that my belly always does what I expect. I mean, sometimes it groans and rumbles, and sometimes it heaves and whines. There's a technical medical term for the sounds it makes, the voices of the belly, a doctor told me it. I can't recall it now, but it's got a name. But I think of it like the sea, my belly. Rising and falling like the tides, like it's linked to some heavenly body the way the tides're linked to the moon. I look at it and ask myself what the hell it's thinking. Like something at the zoo. No sir, you cannot have any more to eat just now! No sir, you're gonna have to last another hour till feeding time! Just you behave!

★

It was during my time at the Ranelagh Grand that I started building this house where I live now. It's timber: timber walls, timber floors. I bought the timber from a yard in

26

Tyler. Timber expands and contracts, and the house creaks in the wind and when the sun shines after rain. I like that, the creaking and the cracking, like the house is alive.

Before this house the land was covered in tumbleweed, and there was nothing much here except a rundown asbestos chicken shack and a track leading down the hill. I paid three hundred dollars for it to a mangy old-timer who looked near enough like a ghost living here since the Civil War or thereabouts. There are odd folk all over, in Drake same as anyplace else, but this old-timer seems to've been real strange. I was told all about him, how he'd sit at the end of the track with a gun in his lap like he was waiting for someone to show up or something, and half-starving dogs hackling up and growling at strangers.

I conversed with him a few times, and he was actually quite interesting. He had this theory he told me about Jesus, how when Jesus was thirty he gave up his body to be occupied by a spirit angel called Melchizedek, and after the Crucifixion Jesus reoccupied his body and went on a kind of worldwide tour. He went to the Red Sea and he caught a ship belonging to Joseph of Arimathea and sailed to New Zealand and the Pacific, and then after a few years the Polynesian islanders paddled him by canoe to South America, and then he traveled up and down South and North America, teaching and healing people. It was a weird theory but, as I say, kind of interesting. This old geezer believed it, anyway. It took him a long time to get it all out, mumbling like his mouth was full of dry gravel. He told me Jesus had probably even been through here, through Drake, not that Drake existed in those days. Then he spat and said, all deadpan, "Came through on the railroad, most prob'ly." That was his kind of joke. He told it like it wasn't a joke but it had to be. "Even if it ain't true," he said to me, "I'm gonna believe it." Yeah, he was weird all right. I don't know what happened to him; after I bought his shack he cleared out and went, dogs and all.

I knocked the shack down, and built this house in its place. I was in no hurry, I took it slow, a good year of sweat and toil. I built it with bedroom, bedroom, bathroom, on the upper floor; kitchen, living room, parlor, bathroom, on the ground floor. Also a porch. I knew what I wanted. Outside I cut back the tumbleweed and planted Texas palm trees and sowed a grass lawn, and round the yard I put a white picket fence to make it look smart, like some big colonial house up in Vermont or somewhere.

The house is set off on the side of a hill without a name. Houses further up the hill but none close enough to trouble you, unless you're that kind of person. I specially liked the house being set by itself and the view down over Drake, on to the C-J Works and the river and the hills beyond. Drake's down in a hollow, you see, like a bowl. Easy enough walking down, more of a toil walking back up, especially as after my shift ended at the Ranelagh Grand, even when I was a bellboy, I used to make a point of checking out the kitchens. There'd be all this top-quality French food prepared by Mr. Tiplady going to waste— good food none of the diners'd happened to order—and I'd stoke up before leaving. Also I used to stop off at

Jackson's, which is a cafe on Willard selling warm donuts and such. It's only half a block beyond the liquor store where Walter Giddins was gunned down. As you walk by, the smell of the donuts drags you in like a fish being netted. I'd get myself a snack there. Beautiful donuts. Nowadays I and Martha get them sent up here, to the house, and they're good as ever.

Those were good times. Sitting at Jackson's after eating donuts and having a game of pinball. Or sitting on the porch in the darkness on a warm summer's night, drinking beer and looking over the picket fence, and the town all spread out like a picnic, and the stars beyond.

Seems a long while off, now. A long, long while. I can't hardly believe it. As I say, they were good times.

Most of the people who stayed at the Ranelagh Grand in my time seemed to be businesspeople, and we often had business conventions for people in the furniture business, and carpet manufacture. Heating engineers. An oil convention once. These conventions would always begin with a reception; then there'd be lectures, in the ballroom. Listening to those I succeeded in gleaning certain good business tips, although at that time I had no notion of going into business. I wasn't ambitious, not at all. I was happy to stay in Drake. The only thought I maybe had was working in New Orleans eventually, but I didn't bother to look too far ahead.

I recall the oil convention well on account of the storms that blew in that weekend. Round here the storm season begins in early spring and runs through to early summer, when for the most part it tapers off. Sometimes, if there's been a dry spring, you may get dust storms off the prairies, and very rarely you have a snow blizzard; there was one right across the Texas Panhandle when I was a kid and none of us could get to school. I recall looking at this fuzzy white stuff and picking it up and chewing it like candy. But that's rare. More common are thunderstorms combined with hail, and maybe a tornado or two thrown in for good measure. This oil convention was held in early April, and the storm came on just as the proceedings were drawing to a close, and the noise of the thunder was so loud it proved impossible to hear the closing address. In the end all the delegates kind of gave up and crowded into the foyer to watch the storm. We get plenty of thunderstorms but what was remarkable about this one was the size and velocity of the hailstones. Some of them must've been big as softballs, not that there was anything soft about them. You could hear them banging down on all the automobiles in the hotel parking lot, battering the metal, smashing the windscreens and the other windows. A crazy oil guy tried running out to his car, I guess with the idea of moving it under cover, but he was beaten back. He was crazy, one of those stones landing on his head might've killed him. It was an awe-inspiring spectacle. Afterward, when the hail eased off, the streets were thick in slushy ice from the melting hail.

Sometimes we had weddings at the Ranelagh Grand, as I say. And sometimes adulterous lovers stayed. You'd get to recognize them from the manner of their behavior toward each other, pawing each other under the dinner tables, that kind of thing. I could tell some stories. Occasionally, a famous person might stay, like a politician, and once we had two Hollywood movie stars, when I was still a bellboy. I recognized them straightaway. They were married but not to each other, and they didn't give their true names when they checked in so I'm not going to embarrass them by naming them, just in case, you never know. But I knew them right away. They got out of this stretch limo, the lady unlacing her legs—that's what it looked like. She was real leggy. Her legs were like kind of silk. She wore dark glasses, mirror glasses; so did the guy. So did the limo, for that matter.

While they were checking in I moved their bags from the limo into the foyer. There were four bags, all very soft, supple leather, pale brown, like from the skin of a baby gazelle. Then Chuck Watson, the hotel manager, who was behind the front desk, handed me the key and said to me, "Room one-two-one," in a manner that suggested he might've recognized them too. One-two-one was one of the best suites, with a queen-size double-poster bed and cathedral ceiling. I lifted the bags, led the way to the waiting elevator, and showed them in. Then I stepped in myself. Squeezed in, you might say. I was pretty large and the elevator was pretty small, and there were the bags as well. We were pressed close against each other. I could smell her perfume, and I felt kind of uneasy, sensing they were looking at me behind their mirror glasses but not knowing where to look myself. I mean I know the ride lasted only a few seconds, but it was real tense. I didn't want to appear prurient, so I looked at the floor of the elevator, at the bags, at her ankles and legs. They were very shapely, the curve of the calves. I recall that, just as the elevator came to a halt, I raised the level of my gaze and saw the tip of her tongue very slightly moving between her lips, moistening her lips, like she might've been about to say something but didn't. Also I saw myself, my own double reflection, squeezed out, distended in the lenses of her glasses.

I led them down the corridor to room one-two-one and unlocked the door, inviting them to enter. They walked inside and I followed, putting down the bags.

"Any more you'd like, any room service, sir?" I asked the man. The lady'd gone straight over to the window.

"No thank you," he said, and put a ten dollar bill in my hand. Then the door closed in my face.

I waited outside for a moment or so, listening, before returning to the elevator. The perfume still hung in the air, and I breathed it in, real deep. A few moments before, that perfume had been on her skin, now it was deep in my lungs.

They didn't call for room service, which was a disappointment. Nor did they use the hotel pool, nor did they come down to dinner, and next day they checked out early, still wearing their dark glasses, though it wasn't what you'd call a bright day. That's what famous movie people do, wear dark glasses on dull days. I guess they wear dark glasses at night, lying in the tub, they probably even wear

32

dark glasses when they're at the movies. It's partly saying they don't want to be recognized but partly saying they do, it's a kind of badge of fame inviting everybody else to guess who they are, like a game. I used to wear dark glasses like that when the business was still running. I reckoned it was a way of kidding people that I was famous, but I don't wear them too much now.

I used to go to the movies, in those days. Drake's got two movie centers, one on Arlington, other on Blythe. But the seats got too tight, I couldn't breathe. The arms digging into me. That's how it is, being this fat. You accept that some things you can't do.

Those two were the first movie stars I'd ever seen in the flesh, however. It was weird. Drake isn't the kind of place you'd bank on seeing movie stars, even if they were being adulterous. Drake's a nowhere place, full of ordinary folk. It doesn't have any Nobel or Pulitzer Prize winners, it doesn't have resident tycoons, it doesn't even have any real what you'd call well-known personalities. Just occasionally you hear the name of someone who used to live in Drake who's now getting nearly famous someplace else, and you think: who's that? I guess the most famous guy you may possibly have heard of would be Larry Reisler, who became a professional golfer. He never was one of the big fish, but he was on the circuit for a time and I believe he won some tournaments early on. He was a left-hander, and he once won himself a Cadillac in a tournament for shooting a hole in one. It was before my arrival in Drake, however, so I'm speaking from

33

hearsay. There's no golf course in Drake, only the Ben Hogan Driving Range, and I don't have any information where Larry Reisler is located now, you don't ever see his name in the *Drake Chronicle* or the *Constant Bulletin*. I guess he's still playing and hoping. If I'm correct he wasn't from Drake but Motson, which is a kind of nothing place about twenty mile up the valley in the Austin direction, and I'm sure folk in Motson could assist if you want to locate him to participate in your project.

You wouldn't say Larry Reisler was ever famous, however. Not famous famous. He never had widespread name recognition, to use Hiram Cutler's phrase. But fame and Drake, as I say, it didn't even sound right together, it was like . . . I don't know. It was like steak and mustard pickle.

★

I can't rightly say how long things might've gone on like this if nothing'd happened. As I say, I wasn't ambitious and I liked the Ranelagh Grand. I might still be there, maybe on the front desk, or maybe at the sister hotel in Austin. Because there's a second Ranelagh Grand, also four stars, in Austin. That was the first Ranelagh Grand, the one in Austin, built about nineteen sixty-two or thereabouts, whereas the Ranelagh Grand in Drake wasn't built until nineteen seventy-three. They were built by a Mr. Leonard Saker, who lived in Austin. He passed away earlier this year, but he used to visit the hotel quite often, and then we had to be smart as hell, you bet. No sir, yes sir, three bags full sir. He was a little bent-back silver-haired man with liver spots, age about eighty or ninety, who used to turn up out of nowhere to check on the hotel. He wasn't really a tycoon, though he did his best to act like one, like he had a silver-tipped cane. He was miserable as hell: he never smiled, or laughed, or frowned much, you never knew what he was thinking. He'd set himself down with his cane in the restaurant in a corner table and order some dish but almost never eat it, just pick at it a moment or two and push it a bit aside with an expression like it tasted like a lump of shit. Sometimes after four or five minutes he'd pull the plate back and take another morsel but sometimes he wouldn't, result being none of the waiters knew when to take the plate away. If they went up and took it too early they were in the wrong, and they were in the wrong if they left it. If they left it too long he'd lift his cane and bring it down hard on the floor. That was the signal to get real worried, yes sir. I was never waitering so I was out of it, and as I recall he never spoke one word to me, but I was still dead scared of him, we all were, even Chuck Watson. He was the manager, even he was scared. It was like we didn't exist. Didn't even seem to register us in his eyes. I guess he meant to scare us, taking one mouthful of food, it was a trick, he was enjoying himself.

Once I remember he found a small spot on one of the linen tablecloths. I don't know why there was a spot, because the cloths were always freshly laundered after being used. I'm all for attention to detail, but this was smaller than one of Mr. Saker's liver spots. But he banged his cane down on the floor for a waiter, and the waiter had to fetch the head waiter and the head waiter had to fetch Chuck Watson, and I don't know what old Saker said but I know he made out it was like some terrible catastrophe had befallen the hotel. Thing is, he was desperate for the Ranelagh Grand to get five-star status. That was his big ambition, that was all he cared about, that's what Chuck Watson told me afterwards. He kept on trying to put in improvements, like the trouser presses. Every room had to have its own trouser press, by order. Then he'd get the lighting changed because it was too low or not too low. Then the taps had to be changed so they were gold, and then he got this idea about Jacuzzi tubs. Every bathroom had to have its Jacuzzi tub, by order Leonard Saker. It was a big thing, it must've cost him a fortune, that's why he was so upset about a spot on the edge of a tablecloth. And every year the inspectors turned up and gave the hotel the same old four-star rating. What did he expect? I mean if old Saker wanted to have a five-star he shouldn't've built a hotel in Drake in the first place. It's just not a five-star kind of place. It's the wrong habitat. I reckon in the end, when the hotel kept on getting the old four stars, he just died of disappointment.

Trouble was, the Ranelagh Grand wasn't always that busy. Sometimes, outside of the convention season, it was real quiet, there'd be scarcely anyone to cook for on a night. The waiters'd lay up all thirty-five tables in the restaurant with the starched white linen cloths and the silver cutlery, and only half a dozen diners'd show up. I didn't mind, looking at it from a personal perspective, as I was able to take my pick of all the food Mr. Tiplady had prepared, but in business terms it was a waste. There was gross underutilization of assets. The unused ballroom, the unslept-in beds, the gold taps that no one bothered to turn, that's not good business.

Even though I was only a lowly member of staff I used to reflect upon this a good deal. My considered view was that the hotel was in the wrong place, that it ought've been in Houston, not Drake, and there was nothing that could've been done about that, but there were other matters that could've been improved on, particularly with regard to marketing. One hot and heavy August night, having left the kitchens, I found myself speaking out on the subject. I was leaving for home, passing the front desk where Mr. Watson was standing, looking out over the marble foyer toward the fountain. If I recall correctly, checking the rack of room keys hanging behind his head, there were maybe only seven rooms occupied, which meant there were sixty-eight vacant. He wished me good night and I returned the greeting, and I then remarked on how quiet the hotel was. He agreed: "Always the same. It's a quiet time of year. Nothing much ever happens this time of year."

"Aside from one or two hailstorms," I said, though tell the truth late summer doesn't see too many storms. I reckon it's too hot, they can't be bothered.

Mr. Watson nodded, and neither of us said anything for

a moment. I was kind of delaying the point when I'd have to leave the cool of the hotel air-conditioning for the heat of the night. When it was hot I dreaded the long walk home, the toil up the hill, it could take me more than an hour. Then I said that maybe in slack periods the hotel ought to offer cut-price deals, to improve occupancy. Something like that.

Chuck Watson seemed kind of surprised; as I say, I was only a lowly member of staff. "Sure," he said, "we could do that, if Mr. Saker wanted it."

"I feel it's a particular pity that the pool's so under-utilized," I said. "It'd be beautiful to have a night swim."

We both sort of stood there, imagining. It was a beautiful big pool. It had marble sides and gold lighting, which gave it a very romantic aura. The lights were kept on all night even though no one ever swam there. That's what I mean about waste.

"Sure," said Mr. Watson. "But it's against the rules, Michael. I can't give you permission."

Up to that point, I hadn't even thought about using the pool myself. My remark was just a general business observation. But that was how Mr. Watson had interpreted it. He continued: "you know, if Mr. Saker found out anyone was in the pool . . . a member of staff . . . they'd be out on their ass. Even if I'd given them permission. I'm not allowed to."

"Is Mr. Saker staying here?" I asked.

"No, but you know what he's like. He never gives any warning, he just shows up."

"At this time of night?"

Chuck Watson gave a shrug, but he seemed to concede that this was probably true. Even old Saker wasn't going to roll in at one in the morning. "It's against the rules," he repeated, "I can't give you permission. If you want to take the risk . . . that's your business. Just so long as you keep me well out of it. I don't know anything about it. I'm going to hit the sack."

He was a good guy, Chuck Watson, he still is. He's been to visit me up here. His son died in a Jet Ski accident when I was still working at the hotel. I was sorry about that. He's no longer at the Ranelagh Grand but down at the Best Western, on Cramer.

Well, he wished me good night, and left me there in something of a quandary. I was pretty tempted to have a swim but I knew I shouldn't. The risk was too great. So I reluctantly went out. But that night was real hot air, the air like glue, and by the time I was halfway up Arlington I was sticky with sweat. I kept thinking of the pool, and I turned round and went back. No one saw me let myself into the hotel. I went past the elevators, turned left, pushed at the pool door. It was locked but I could see, through the window, the water glistening like gold. And I knew where the key was hung behind the front desk.

I fetch the key and go in. Turn off the lights, slip off my clothes. The tiles are cool to my bare feet. Then I lower myself over the side, into the deep end, naked and silent as possible, and let myself float out. It's wonderful. Not just on account of the change of temperature, which makes my body give a kind of inner sigh, but because the water bears me up and all the weight slides off me in an instant. I could be no weight at all. Fetal? Like being in the womb, the amniotical fluid? That's what the psychoanalysts'd say. I don't know. I don't know. But, on such a hot night, it was more pleasurable than I know how to describe properly. I hadn't swum since I was a kid, when I swam in Lake Constant, but now I roll and float and drift, mostly on my back, occasionally sculling with my hands, until I get near the filter. Then I lower my legs and hold on to the side and feel the current bubbling and coursing round my groin like cool fingers. Later I push out again, and the pool seems deep as imagination, and I feel myself rising above the water, almost floating, like I've lost my body completely.

Well, that first occasion, I didn't stay long. Ten minutes, no more. But there were others. Night after night I went back, secretly, I couldn't stop myself. It wasn't just refreshing, like a drink of soda: the experience gave me strength, like I was bathing in some magic river. Least, that was what I felt. I knew that if I was caught there'd be serious consequences, I'd be out on my ass as Mr. Watson'd said, but I was young, and on nights when the temperature was over eighty-five and the humidity ninety-six or ninety-seven I couldn't resist. What I reckoned was that if I was ever challenged I could bluff my way out by saying I was one of the guests.

Came the night when, as I was wallowing in the pool, two hotel guests showed up, a man and a woman. One of

40

the honeymoon couples maybe. They didn't turn on the lights, which was fortunate, and I kept still. In retrospect keeping still was a poor idea because soon enough after jumping in and swimming in circles round each other and laughing they started to kiss and fondle each other. Obviously they had no idea of anyone else being in the pool. I was up at the deep end but my eyes were well enough adjusted to the darkness, and what I couldn't see for sure I made up in imagination. They started about halfway down from the shallow end, in the middle of the pool, but then they moved to the side. She was right against the side and he hoisted her up and she wrapped her legs round him. Soon she was making little choking noises and crying: "Oh jeez . . . oh jeez . . . shit no . . . " almost like she was whimpering.

Now I was very naïve about these matters. Being so fat, I'd no sexual experiences myself, not even a kiss. I was the virgin of virgins. But being in the pool with them, in the same water, it felt like I was part of it too. I became very aroused as the woman's cries came quicker and quicker. The man was grunting hard. When they finished the woman swam in a steady breaststroke towards the deep end, where I was. She passed close without apparently noticing me, but there was a luminescence about her naked body like you might get about the body of a fish. I imagined the sperm leaking out of her, I felt the wash as she swam by. I was very aroused, as I say.

It was after that I began to search out sexual experience for myself. In particular one of the chambermaids became the subject of my lustful desire. I'm not going into it in detail, but she was quite old and fat, sagging all over, with dark Indian skin and a nose like a hawk's, and she had something wrong with her lower lip as if she'd been in some accident, but of all the chambermaids she was the one appealed to me most. Mr. Saker insisted the chambermaids wore little black dresses with white frilly aprons, and I used to lie awake at night not able to sleep and sweating with desire at the thought of catching her in one of the elevators or as she was making up one of the beds in the mornings. I thought of hitching up that dress and planting my hands on her fat haunches as she bent over the bed. I also thought of riding up and down with her in the elevator from the first floor to the seventh and back again, up and down and up and down, pressing the button to keep the doors closed. It was crazy since I'd barely spoken to her, and nor did I have much opportunity to, as I was working in the kitchens while she was in the bedrooms, and she worked mornings and I didn't have any reason to get into the hotel until noon. However, in the hope of making her acquaintance better, I took to showing up early. I'd walk around the hotel like I had some important business to conduct, such as checking the fire alarms, and happen to meet her, as if by chance, and by this means I came to exchange more words with her. I guess that she must have noticed how I'd often be hanging about her as she worked.

One morning I got early to the hotel as she was about to get into one of the elevators. She was pushing a trolley loaded with fresh clean laundry, and carrying a broom.

"Good morning," I said, squeezing in. It was a tight fit.

"Good morning." She had a key in one hand and the broom in the other. She pressed the button for the third floor and up we went. "How're you doing today?"

I said I was just fine.

"You're sure in early," she said, and I thought her eyes were running over me in a speculative manner. But I didn't dare meet her eyes. I just looked at her fat legs beneath the black skirt and white apron.

"Yeah," I said, "things to do."

The doors opened and she got out, and I got out. She began pushing her trolley along to the room she was cleaning, I think it was three-two-seven. When she got there she tried the door but it wasn't locked, and she went in while I continued to the end of the corridor. I pretended to check on the fire door. Then I came back again. She was stripping the sheets off the unmade bed. "Feel like helping?" she asks, and I came into the room. Next thing I knew, she was all over me, almost kind of rapacious, hauling at my pants, pulling me down on her. It wasn't anything like I'd imagined. Her face was contorted. Her hawk nose seemed like a beak. She looked older than my ma, she looked about ninety-five. I was filled with revulsion, not only at her but at myself. I tore away and left, fast as I could.

After this she started to haunt me round the hotel. She'd wait beyond the end of her shift for my arrival in order to strike up conversation or worse if she had a chance, forcing herself on me, despite my protestations and evident

43

revulsion, and she even pursued me into the kitchens. I told her to leave me alone but she paid no attention till Mr. Tiplady threw her out after a pan of water was knocked over. Mr. Tiplady was a big cheerful guy if you kept on the right side of him, but he didn't like anyone in his kitchens without express permission. He didn't even like Mr. Watson coming in when he was cooking. When the pan of boiling water went over he uttered a roar like an angry lion, and physically evicted her telling her never to enter the kitchens again. Thereafter the kitchens became, for a number of weeks, my place of refuge and safety. It was embarrassing, nonetheless, since Mr. Tiplady obviously reckoned I and this horny old chambermaid were pretty deeply involved with each other, and he taunted me a good deal to that effect, to the amusement of the rest of the kitchen staff, who proceeded to chip in and taunt me in their turn. There were many remarks passed, often quite crude in nature, relating to the sexual acts we had supposedly committed on each other. The more I protested the more taunting I came in for, till I didn't know what to do. But I knew I only had myself to blame. Tell the truth, I'd made a pretty big fool of myself.

★

I guess by now you'll be thinking the reason I was fired from the Ranelagh Grand was on account of some subsequent sexual misdemeanor or my illicit use of the swimming pool coming to the notice of Mr. Saker. In fact it was something else entirely. One day, I fell through the bathroom floor. Not at the Grand, but here at home.

Okay, I knew the dangers. I'd already stepped through the porch, and though I was much lighter than I am now, I was getting heavier and fatter all the time. I didn't weigh myself, but I could tell by the way my clothes weren't fitting me anymore. My shirts and pants kept on tearing. And the timber floor used to groan if I stepped on it. When I went upstairs, therefore, as a precautionable measure, I used to take two pieces of square timber with me, to spread the load. I'd use them like stepping stones across a river: I'd stand on one and push the other ahead of me, and stand on it; then reach down and pick up the one I'd been standing on. It wasn't always so easy, keeping my balance while picking it up. If you're very fat, bending down is kind of awkward.

This time I lost my balance and my weight went down on the boards. I felt myself going straight through and flung myself forward, but I went between the joists and crashed through to the room where I am now. My ankle snapped like a rotten twig. I even heard it snapping, the snap of the bone. I guess I was lucky not to break my neck. And I was real lucky to be near a telephone.

The rescue wasn't easy. First there were only two ambulance crewmen came. They took one look at me, covered in dust and plaster, and sent for reinforcements. So there were four ambulance men, and they couldn't shift me either, and they had to call up another four to get me upright. They were nice guys. They stood around scratching their chins

45

and mulling the matter over. For a while it looked like I might be stuck where I was into perpetuity or the sounding of the last trumpet, you might say.

News spread; I can't rightly say how. Drake's like Constant, it's the kind of place in which news spreads like an infectious disease, and some guy showed up with a camera. I didn't know who he was. These stretcher men were standing round scratching their chins and every now and then giving me a heave, and this guy lines up with his camera! Next week what do I know, but there's this big photograph on the front page of the *Drake Chronicle*, with a caption that describes me as the Colossus of Drake. I was amused by that, the Colossus of Drake. The Colossus of Drake. First time I'd ever seen myself in those terms. They'd even put alongside it a smaller picture, of the original Colossus, from ancient times.

The article in the *Drake Chronicle*, and accompanying photograph, did not make me famous. Of course not. Not even well known, even if it was on the front page. But if fame's a rare, exotic perfume, like the perfume of that movie star in the elevator, I guess you'd say that article gave me a little sniff. I had it in my nostrils. I was famous in Drake for a week, you'd say, till the next issue of the *Chronicle*.

While my ankle knit I couldn't work at the hotel, so I went back home to Constant. My ma cared for me. She set up a bed in the parlor. I was there some months. If you carry as much weight as I do, you have to take care not to test a fragile joint until it's ready. And while I was convalescing and being unable to walk about and eating my ma's food like a turkey fattening itself up for the knife at Thanksgiving I didn't move about so much, and I put on more flesh. It arrived, almost from nowhere, like a blessing or a curse, whatever, like nothing under the sun. When my ankle broke I reckon I was still no more than four hundred pounds but after three months at home I guess I was more than six hundred. It's hard to say for sure, it's only a guess. That was what they reckoned at the San Antonio Clinic. In a few weeks I'd gone and picked up two hundred pound of flesh!

The San Antonio Clinic was where I went to have my ankle treated, and the doctors and nurses there were always bugging me about my weight. Saying I should have died long ago. Saying being fat as I was was too much of a strain on the heart. Too much strain on the heart, the liver, the limbs. Though they never used the word fat, they said "obese." The medical term. I was suffering from gross obesity, severe obesity, morbid obesity, super obesity. Probably the whole lot altogether.

It was there I was diagnosed with diabetes mellitus. They took a urine test and a blood test and several other tests and then they told me, diabetes mellitus. When they first told me I imagined I'd be injecting myself with a syringe, like a drug addict. I couldn't bear that idea. I mean even finding a vein to inject wouldn't be so easy, and putting the needle into yourself . . . thank you but no. But then they said it was type two diabetes, so I wouldn't need the injections. That was what the nurse said and I

47

was pretty reassured. She said the most important thing was eating in a regular fashion. But the doctors weren't reassuring at all. One doctor was the worst, his name was Griffith. He kept hauling me back into his office and trying to frighten me, telling me about the long-term complications of diabetes mellitus, trying to persuade me I was already halfway to the morgue.

"D'you ever feel dizzy?"

"Not especially."

"Hmmmm . . . " —like he didn't believe me— "D'you tremble?"

"No. Not especially."

"Hold out your hand."

I held out a hand and of course it trembled. "It doesn't bother me," I said.

He went on like I hadn't spoken. "Do you ever experience numbness in your feet, or hands?"

I said "no" again, though it wasn't entirely true. It depends what you mean by numbness. At the time I used to get what you might call a certain tingling, not what I called true numbness.

"And you're—how old?"

He knew that, he had my medical notes in front of him. But I told him anyway. "Twenty." That's how old I was then.

"Twenty years old, and you're six hundred and forty-five pounds," he said. "Would you please tell me what you eat, on an average day? A typical day. Take me through it, from the moment you wake up in the morning."

I took him through it. He made notes as I spoke. He

48

kept frowning. "So, a vast quantity of fat and carbo-hydrate," he said at last, with an air of distaste.

"I don't reckon it's that much," I said.

He checked his notes. "Four or five pizzas. Four burgers. Four loaves of bread. Four sacks of fries. Twelve donuts."

"I'm a big man," I said. "You want me to stop eating? How long for?"

"How long do you want to live? That's the question you need to ask yourself. Unless you get down to a viable bodyweight, you will die."

He brought this out with a kind of flourish, almost like he was pleased to be saying it. I said to him, "Sure I'm going to die sometime. Who isn't? It's a fact of the human condition."

"You'll die sooner than you think, if you go on like this," he replied. "You could die next month, next week, tomorrow. You're on death row, Michael! You're under sentence of imminent execution!"

That was what he was like—real ghoulish. No thought of trying to make me feel better about myself, he just wanted to scare me.

He crossed his legs. I remember that. He crossed them and leaned forward in a chatty, fireside manner, like he was the President or something. I could see what was coming, he was about to give me a shot of sincerity. "Tell me, Michael," he said, "tell me, d'you enjoy being obese?"

"I am what I am," I say. "It's not a choice. That's how I'm made. I accept it."

"Oh, we are all constrained by heredity to a degree,"

he answered. "But that doesn't mean we can't do anything to change ourselves, does it? Michael, your real problem is obesity. That's what's causing your diabetes. The diabetes is secondary. And if we want to get on top of your diabetes, we need to address the fundamental problem, which is that of weight. Believe me, Michael, it's your only long-term chance. I'm not sure that we would be willing to treat your diabetes unless you also allowed us to treat your obesity. The two go hand in hand."

I wish I could imitate his voice. It was very precise, like he talked with punctuation, like he was writing. I didn't say anything. I let him go on.

"We need to work out a proper program of weight reduction for you. Don't worry, don't get alarmed. We'll make it easy for you. We'll give you medication which will suppress your feelings of hunger. If necessary we can go one step further and wire your jaws together. You'll be able to drink fluids, naturally."

"How'd I talk with my jaws wired?"

"You can communicate. You'll find ways."

He was already talking like I'd agreed!

"Is this what you usually recommend for diabetic patients?"

"Of course not." He was really relaxed by now, he was really enjoying himself. He clasped his hands round his crossed knees. "You are a special case, Michael. In fact, I can say with some certainty, you are by some considerable distance the most obese individual whom I have encountered in my entire career."

I was still trying to come to terms with what he'd said a moment earlier. "You want to wire up my jaws!?"

"Well, there are alternative, or complementary, strategies. For instance, a simple operation whereby we can reduce the length of your digestive tract so that you'll absorb less food. Or, and I think this is what I'd advise, if we decide to rule out wiring, we can reduce the size of your stomach so you'll feel full sooner. It's known as gastroplasty. And over time . . . with determination . . . with willpower . . . I think you would achieve substantial weight reduction, Michael. I don't think everyone could do it. They wouldn't have the strength of character. But I think you could do it. I know you could do it."

I didn't say anything for a moment. All I could think of was how many dollars this guy would be making out of me, wiring me up and reducing the size of my stomach. What would it cost? One thing you find if you're obese, especially if you're obese like me, you can't get health insurance coverage. It's the same for Martha, same for anyone over three hundred pounds, no one'll cover you. It's discrimination. They say you're too high a risk. I guess it's the same if you're too thin or too tall or short, if you don't fit into the social parameters of what is considered normal, no one wants to know. No sir thank you! Well thank you too, for nothing! It's not as though it's my fault that I'm obese. That's how I am, it's how I've been made by Providence. I'm not angry, I've come to accept it, that's how things are, but I don't reckon it's right.

I asked this Dr. Griffith how much it'd cost, and I don't

remember exactly what he told me. He gave a kind of vague answer, not wanting to be pinned down. That's what quacks always do. What I do recall was thinking how, while I was wired up and starving, he'd be taking a vacation at my expense, lying on some beach in the Bahamas!

I said, "How would you reduce the size of my stomach?"

His hand described an airy gesture. "Again, there are possibilities that we'd need to explore, to find out which would be most appropriate in your case. The most suitable course, I think, would be a matter of stapling."

That did it. Stapling! Don't talk to me about stapling! I knew all about stapling from the C-J Works! I could just imagine my belly punctured by staples. Jesus!

Sure, I'm inventing. We had several conversations and I couldn't swear to our words being exactly like that. But he was a sour old guy, that doctor Griffith. A quack. Trying to tell people how to live their lives, is that what a doctor's meant to do? Correct me if I'm wrong, but as I understand it doctors have a duty to cure sickness, and I wasn't sick. I was fat, okay, but I wasn't sick! Fatness isn't a disease in itself, is it? It may be a condition, but it's not a disease. It's not like diabetes mellitus. That's what I was trying to say about the insurance. If there's a single thing I'd like to say on these tapes, it is that being fat or being heavy is not a sickness. This is the greatest misapprehension society has about very fat people such as myself, it's the basis for the stigmatization that exists and that I myself was very soon to directly experience at the sharp end when I was fired from the Ranelagh Grand for being too fat!

The fat, or the heavy, are a tiny minority group, and like other minorities suffer a degree of persecution and misunderstanding at the hands of the majority. They have their rights, however, as enshrined in the Constitution laid down by this nation's founding fathers. Though I don't give interviews any longer, there is a certain side of me that says heavy people like myself with access to the media have a duty to promote and publicize the situation in which ordinary heavy people find themselves. That's one reason why I'm taking part in your project.

Going back to this doctor, Dr. Griffith, I reckon he was medically wrong. I'm not saying he was medically incompetent or anything like that, but six summers ago he said I'd be dead and I'm still alive. I'd like to meet him again and look him straight in the eye, and tell him how very healthy I feel, yes sir, thank you for your kind inquiry. And I do. Health is in the mind, not in the body. My mind is alive and flourishing, thank you. I trouble to keep it so. That's why I'm alive, I guess.

I'm not sure what else I need to tell you. When my ankle was better I came back to Drake, and my life continued much as before, though I stopped going up the stairs. I realized I was too heavy to take the risk, and I just lived downstairs. But I was pleased to be back home; I mean I've always liked it here. The house has windows facing east and west and south, and though I can't see the sunrise on account of the hill, I see the sunset. We get beautiful sunsets round here. I love the sunsets, looking west, thinking of all that land out west the sun is still shining on while its last rays are leaving Drake.

I need to take a break now, but before I do I'd like to say, looking back over my experiences, how I do reckon Providence has been with me all the time, planning everything on my behalf, like a guiding hand. Almost like my life's been a dream. That's how I feel tonight, anyway, not for any reason. It's just another summer night. I've eaten some pizza, drunk some beer, fed the cat, talked with Martha on the telephone . . . washed and powdered myself. That's very important if you're fat, powdering yourself, to prevent chafing. And now the windows are open and I feel the breeze on my skin, and listen to the sounds of the railroad across the valley. I know what's going to happen in a few minutes, it's always the same. The train pulling in from Austin to the depot. The doors opening, folk getting on and off, then the doors slamming shut. Then there's a hoot, and the train's setting off for Constant, and I hear the rattle of wheels turning faster and faster and in my mind I follow the lights of the train as it climbs out of Drake and disappears along the plain towards the Blue Falls. You can hear it a long time on a night like this, but gradually the sound'll diminish, like a fading image, like a star fading into the dark of the night, till I'm only hearing it in tiny little snatches, not sure if I'm hearing it or just imagining it, till I know I'm not hearing it any longer. Then the silence falls. It's gone. But even then, even then, I'm still watching the train, I'm watching that line of lighted wagons moving along the railroad, over the darkened face of the earth.

Those are the times I like best, the darkness, and the sound of the railroad, and the ensuing silence. It opens some kind of wide space in my mind. I think of my pa sawing and stroking wood, and the Blue Falls roaring on for ever and ever. I can't explain it as well as I'd wish to, but it's those times, in the darkness, I feel most free. It's something like my idea of death. I can't explain it exactly, but it's those times I feel most free.

2

Michael is aged twenty, but he could be any age from twenty to sixty. He almost defies description in conventional terms; his appearance is so unlike that of any human being whom you have ever met, or dreamed of meeting, that he seems altogether alien, a member of some entirely different species. When you ring the doorbell of the home in Drake, Texas, where he lives, alone, and semi-reclusive, you wait a long time before hearing the sound of his approach. Even that has a heavy, subterranean quality, as of some mythical monster out of the pages of Ancient Greek literature dragging its unwieldy form through its passageways of its darkened lair. In the words of Ireland's great bard, W. B. Yeats, what rough beast slouches here? Then the door opens. It is a paralyzing moment. This figure, this giant, this hulk of hulks, this man-mountain, looms before you, wearing a pale and voluminous robe and a pair of baggy short pants above bare feet, and holding out something that's both strange and familiar. What can it be? You realize: it's a hand. He's holding out his hand, on the end of a baggy spar that must be an arm. The realization sends a shiver down your spine. You don't know whether to laugh or cry, or flee. You take the hand with trepidation, with awe, with the sense that you are shaking hands with History. This is surely the hand of the heaviest man in the United States. He may be the heaviest man in the world. He may even be the heaviest man ever.

Then comes this voice, which is an incredible revelation. Because it's reedy. The voice of a thin man! It comes from this opening in the face, which must be a mouth.

The face is extraordinary. The eyes seem tiny, so engulfed are they by the surrounding acreage of flesh. However, it is at the chin and neck, a neck which no longer exists in any meaningful sense of the word, that Michael's corpulence truly begins to assert itself. The chins, and he has maybe half a dozen, lie one on the other like layers of pale, uncooked pastry dough prepared by some master baker. The other comparison which springs most forcibly to mind, however, is that of candle wax.

At my request, he consents to part his robe. Momentarily, I am literally dumbstruck. His breasts are so flabby they're saddlebags. They slop to his belly, and the belly is truly something beyond comprehension. Not so much because of its size, although over the years it has been stretched by the force of gravity to a creature of stupendous dimensions, but because of its fluidity and flaccidity. When he attempts to stand, it rests upon the floor, and its weight is so great that it pulls him into a stoop. When he reclines on his beanbags (he no longer sleeps on a bed, because no bed frame can support his weight, just as he no longer dares tread up the stairway), it sprawls and flows gently away from him with the motion of molasses.

We go into the living room. He moves ahead of me, his thick sides and steatopygous buttocks brushing the walls. He's not exactly walking, and he's not even waddling; each of his legs is so fat that it fatally impedes the progress of the other, and instead he locomotes by dragging himself along, using his arms to heave his body forward and reminding me irresistibly of the reptilian gait of some antediluvian creature like a stegosaur.

We talk about himself. He's articulate, quite intelligent and soft-spoken, in this squeaky little voice that seems curiously at odds with his size. He is an avid reader, who loves the works of John Steinbeck, and a deeply knowledgeable fan of country music. He believes strongly in God. Born in 1958 in the little cotton town of Constant, Michael's childhood ambition was to be a railroad driver. He has little understanding of his unique- ness. When I ask him what it feels like to be the fattest man in America, he answers: "I don't know it feels so different. One man's fat, another man's thin."

In answer to the matter of why he's so fat, Michael replies: "I believe it's Providence. Providence made me fat."

Yet all the time that he's talking, in that thin reedy voice of his, I cannot take my eyes off of the monstrosity of his belly.

That's part of what she wrote, the art writer. She came to see me in the summer of seventy-eight. In the winter of nineteen seventy-seven I'd been contacted by a Houston-based photographer by the name of Eddie Dukes. He had heard about me in consequence of the *Chronicle* article, and he laid before me a proposition: would I be willing to pose for photographs? To his certain knowledge, he said, no professional had ever photographed someone as fat as me before.

The proposition seemed harmless enough; I didn't bother to check him out or anything. Naïve? Sure. I was naïve then. But I've got nothing to say against Eddie Dukes.

He was a small neatish guy with sandy hair, and sallow skin covered in freckles. He wore a black leather jacket and a gold bangle round his wrist and these slick Indian-moccasin-type shoes, mottled, like they'd been skinned off a snake's back. I'd love shoes like that. Tell the truth, my feet being so fat I hardly ever wear any shoes, not proper shoes, just some bits of soft leather laced together.

I'd got my smart clothes out for him but he didn't want that; he said he wanted me to wear whatever I wore bumming round the place by myself. So I changed. He looked at me.

"D'you have a string vest? Could you wear that?"

As he'd come all the way from Houston I didn't want

to disappoint him, so I put the string vest on. He set up his tripod and photographed me half the day, on my beanbags, washing dishes, drinking beer, yawning and stretching, combing my hair in a mirror. He took shots of me face on, back on, side on, you name it; I couldn't believe how many shots the guy was taking.

"This is some use to you, is it?"

"Michael," he said, "if I'm not wasting your time, you're not wasting mine."

He even took a shot of me lathering up. I had to lather up and shave specially for him, though I'd already shaved that morning. I pretended to shave. He seemed pleased enough, but it was difficult to say for sure.

"You're the fattest man I've ever seen," he said. "I seen some fat people but you're the fattest. You're the fattest man in America?"

I said that I didn't know.

"Reckon you might be," he said. "I'll check it out."

I didn't hear a thing from him for months after that. Then I got an invitation to this photographic exhibition in Savannah. It was called "The Fattest Man in America," so I knew I was. A promo leaflet was included. It had a long piece about Mr. Dukes and his pioneering work documenting the life of small-town America, and how he was much influenced by Edward Hopper, an artist I hadn't heard of just then. The promo also showed some of the photographs, and they were all black and white. That surprised me, I couldn't understand why he hadn't done them in color, and tell the truth I confess to being disappointed. In that sweaty string vest, lying on my beanbags, with my belly flopping in front of me, I looked a terrible sight! I couldn't figure out why he hadn't let me wear a shirt and tie, as I'd meant to do. And in the shaving photo a blob of foam had fallen down onto my chest.

Well: I didn't go to Savannah. I know it's meant to be a pretty historic place and all that, but I couldn't fit in an ordinary car and I couldn't see how to get there. I wasn't sure if I wanted to go, either; in some kind of way, I regretted those photographs.

Still, I told my ma, and the next thing I know, she's driving off to the exhibition. Partly as an excuse, I guess, to see my Uncle Vince, her brother. He lives in Wilmington, up the coast from Savannah. He's a nightclub supervisor. That evening, she calls me on the phone from the Savannah hotel in which she's staying. Everyone likes the photographs, she says, they're great, and when folk'd heard that she was my mother, they were all over her. I said, "How'd they know who you were?"

"I told them," she said. "My! Ain't you dumb sometimes, Michael!"

She was in a daze. They'd given her glasses of champagne. They'd *serenaded* her! "I'm so proud," she kept on saying. "I just wish your pa was alive now. I just wish your pa was alive." And that was nice, because I hadn't in all honesty ever done much of anything before she could've been proud of.

Now this art writer, I suppose she was an art writer.

She was something to do with Eddie Dukes. What she told me was the exhibition was so successful it was going on tour. It had secured rock-solid commercial backing and negotiations were taking place with gallery owners round the States. She had been commissioned to write a profile of me—I believe she called it an appreciation—for a catalogue. Well, she stayed for an hour or so and gave me a grilling about things, and later she sent me the copy.

I recall reading it for the first time. Previous, I hadn't met some of the words she used, like steatopygous. Steatopygous, I had to ask someone what it meant. It means "fat-buttocked." So what she actually wrote was, I had fat-buttocked buttocks. I mean, that's just showing off, using a word like that. As for my voice being so very thin and reedy, does it sound like that to you?

How about this? Talking deep.

Reedy.

However.

However, for the rest of it, I did feel kind of flattered. Some of the things I loved, like how I was deeply knowledgeable about country music and an avid fan of John Steinbeck. But I'd possibly have been flattered whatever she'd written. I mean, having an article written about you in an art magazine! Then this tour. Tell the truth, I didn't really give much credence to that, I even toyed with the thought she was spinning me a line.

Well, I was wrong. Wrong as I could be. The exhibition toured the great cities of the United States, it visited

Chicago, New York, Boston, Washington, Houston, and Los Angeles, and wherever it went it pulled in the crowds like a bear being pulled into a cache of honey. In two weeks in New York it pulled in more than four thousand viewers. People were truly fascinated. If I had to hazard an opinion, and you must recall I didn't actually set eyes on the exhibition, I'd put its popularity partly down to the big-size photographs. Six feet by nine feet, that kind of size, they made a proper visual impact.

Much more important, and I guess this lies behind any successful business venture, would be smart marketing. The exhibitions were well promoted in every sense of the word. "The Fattest Man in America," it's the kind of title that grasps you by the throat. Grabs you by the throat I should say. That's the kind of title I want for my business manual. Having said that, I would be the first to acknowledge the truth of the saying that all the marketing in the world is of no use if the product is wrong.

At the time, back here in Drake, I confess that I experienced mixed feelings about the exhibition's success. Sure, I felt a degree of reflected glory, but I was never identified except as Michael. And I myself was making not a single dime out of it all. When Mr. Dukes called on me the commercial potential of the photographs never crossed my mind.

I mentioned how after I busted my ankle and went back to live in Constant I lost my employment at the Ranelagh Grand. Mr. Watson called me in, on the orders of Mr. Saker.

He was pretty apologetic, tell the truth, he didn't want to fire me. "I've got no option," he kept on saying, "it's not my decision." First he told me that my old position in the kitchens had been filled. I offered to work in another capacity, thinking maybe I could work behind the front desk, or as pool attendant. At this Mr. Watson looked real uneasy. "Fact is," he said at last, "it's Mr. Saker says you've got to leave. He finds your size objectionable."

"What?"

"He doesn't like it. It's a matter of image, Michael. He says it's bad for the image of a hotel like the Ranelagh Grand."

"But no one sees me if I work in the kitchens."

"I'm sorry, Michael. It's the five stars again. The inspectors might look in the kitchens. They might see you as a safety hazard."

"A safety hazard?" I couldn't quite take this in. "That what Mr. Saker says? I'm unsafe? Why'm I unsafe?"

"I'm sorry." He did look pretty uneasy. He's a nice guy.

But it was bad news. People have to eat proportionate to their size; if you're my size, you eat a quantity, and it costs a lot of dollars. I'd got a few savings, having been brought up to value financial prudence, but a man with one bad eye could've seen I needed to acquire a source of income fast. I thought about truck driving or security work, I made a few inquiries. I tried the railroad again, but it was the same as before. I even tried the old C-J Works. This was the hot steamy season, I was dripping sweat, and every time, soon as they saw me, it was the same old thing: "Sorry, you're too darn fat, you're too heavy." They didn't always put it like that. They'd say something like, "We have a small concern about your personal appearance."

I resented it at the time, but I don't resent it now. I guess it's true, my body was telling me I'd outgrown ordinary employment.

My pa used to say that it's when a man's down you can tell what he's made of. And there's something else he'd say: "If you throw your bread on the water, it'll come back buttered." I began to rethink. I stocktook. I faced up to facts. That woman art writer's article was the one that did it. That line about my uniqueness. It suddenly struck me how my body was unique like one of my pa's chairs. It was a creation, an artifact, a product.

So I threw out a slice of bread on the water. I put a big box advertisement in the columns of the *Drake Chronicle*. It cost twenty-five dollars. I recall it now. It read:

PHOTOGRAPH THE FATTEST
MAN IN AMERICA

SATURDAYS 10:00 AM–5:00 PM, local time

$2.00 a snap

DON'T MISS!

Then my address, of course.

That first Saturday, as ten o'clock drew near, I waited in some trepidation. Was I nervous? You bet. I'd done no market research, no nothing, I was gambling on a hunch based only on the success of that photographic exhibition. I can't say, in all honesty, I was that confident. Still if no one came, I wasn't going to lose too much. I don't reckon I truly believed anyone'd show up.

How many? Guess. Answer's fourteen. Fourteen people came. (And four of those were kitchen staff from the Ranelagh Grand, come to snigger.) Still, fourteen was fourteen, and even Nelson D. Rockefeller had to start someplace. I welcomed them. They were interested, curious, I guess. Some photographed me. One or two prodded me, even. When this happened, the first time, I was astonished. This man was with these two boys, his sons I guess, and one of them—one of the boys—asked if he could touch.

."Ray!" said the father.

"I don't mind," I said. "Touch if you want, Ray."

So he put out a finger and touched some of the flesh around my . . . my midriff, I guess you'd call it. My belly. At first gingerly, then harder.

His father said, "What does it feel like, Ray?"

The boy laughed. "Soft. Fat. Kinda—"

"What?"

"Kinda how you'd expect."

Then his brother pressed me, and the father too. The father actually squeezed. He took a load of flesh in his mitt and squeezed.

He said to me, as they left, "Thank you sir. We're most grateful."

"Not at all," I said.

"It's been a privilege. Yes sir." He was really respectful.

On another Saturday a young couple, on vacation from Maryland, had this little newborn baby with them. It was a cute thing, boy or girl I couldn't say, with this crumpled-up red face, and they got me to cradle it in my arms for a photograph. They were real pleased; it makes me pleased even now, recalling that, it was cute.

Now, as I look back on those early days, I feel a real stab of shame at my amateurism. I had no formal business training or experience and I admit that when those first visitors came I wasn't properly prepared. I hadn't considered how I should behave, or dress, or compose myself; I hadn't considered the structure of the event; I hadn't worked out what to do if a load of people showed up at the same time. In any business venture one must decide on the appropriate strategy in relation to the customer or client, and that I had dismally failed to do.

Thus I greeted the visitors as would a host with guests, and offered to answer any reasonable questions that they wished to put to me. It wasn't the right strategy. They were often embarrassed and self-conscious, and once they'd taken their photos and put a few halting questions to me there was nothing else for them to do. The end of their visit, when I had to ask them to pay, was the most awkward point. I was only charging two dollars a photograph but I felt a little guilty charging anything at all.

Fact is, though I'd put two dollars a photograph in the *Chronicle*, it always ended up at a flat two dollars however many photographs they took.

It was a month or two before I worked round to the fact that I would need someone else to introduce the visitors to the house and to take their money. I couldn't make the project work on my own. But I was in no real position, financially, to become an employer. I had no financial buoyancy. Sure, I might've taken out a bank loan. But the enthusiasm vital to the success of any business venture surely has to be tempered by a degree of prudence, and the only collateral I'd be able to lay down was my property. If the business foundered, and I lost my property, I'd be lost. Besides, who knew if any bank manager would have been farsighted enough to bankroll me?

Another saying of my pa was that when you need true help you turn to your family first, and I turned to my ma. She'd arrive on Friday, either by car, if it hadn't broken down again, or morning train, and stay till Sunday morning. She'd get a cab up from the railroad; she's no walker. I'd hear the train approaching from Constant and a few minutes later see this cab coming up the track in a haze of dust with my ma beaming away. Then she'd be unpacking what she'd brought, food and often clothes. She made this beautiful purple velvet robe with gold braid trim for me to wear during the viewings. That's what we called them, the viewings. I loved the robe. She's a good seamstress, my ma, and when I was wearing it I felt like a king. Didn't have no buttons because if you've got very fat fingers buttons aren't good news, nor poppers either, instead it had this cord tie.

The next year she moved in and became my full-time manager. She ran the place. Did the groceries, helped with cooking, received the viewers, organized me. Because I never was an organized kind of person. My sister Hilary, she's organized. She lives up in Richmond, California, with this university guy who has little gold-rimmed glasses and a bald head. He's a dinosaur hunter. He goes down to Arizona and places and digs up fossilized dinosaurs, or something, anyway. They've got two little kids, Frank and Anita, whom I've never seen though I'd like to, but California . . . California's a long way off and traveling's another big problem for fat and heavy people. Austin and Fort Worth've both got airports but I couldn't fly. Couldn't even fit through most airplane doorways, I guess! I've never been in an airplane, but I've seen pictures enough to know how tight the space is. No, if I wanted to go to California I'd have to go by hired truck.

My ma's presence enabled me to take on a more passive role, in which I would sit or lie on my beanbags, wearing a robe and exposing quantities of flesh; after all, that was, as I now appreciated, what viewers had come to see. They wanted to see flesh, and as much of it as decently possible. They wanted to be able to photograph it. Flesh, pure and simple, the allure of flesh. I would still answer questions, but when I did so I was less free and easy than I had been and confined myself very much to factual matters. I encouraged people to touch me, with this notice: GENTLE

TOUCHING PERMITTED. People always touched me. Particularly the women, I may say. Particularly the women. Put a finger on my side. Or stroked slightly. Like touching and stroking a rare ornament. If they wanted to touch me, if it gave them pleasure, who was I to object?

Some of the women wanted to go further, they wanted me to sling an arm round them or to kiss me on the cheek, and there were two young women showed up one Saturday whispering to each other for a moment before asking—blushing and giggling—if they could sit in my lap to be photographed. I said, "Go ahead—one at a time," and the first one snuggles in, wriggling slightly, squirming, like she's trying to discover the most comfortable position, and throwing an arm round my neck while the other takes a snap. Then they exchange places. They were both pretty attractive young women and I was in hog heaven, well, tell the truth I was at risk of becoming aroused, which might've been embarrassing if they'd happen to've detected the fact. I reckon maybe they knew that. What appealed to them was the potential danger of the situation.

I should say in those days I never felt there was anything wrong about what I was doing. You see there's another saying: If life gives you lemons, make lemonade. That's all I was doing. Life had made me fat and I was making the most of it, that's all.

★

Now, thinking back, I guess it mightn't've happened but for the Burgerland Museum Experience. That was what was sitting in the back of my mind. It doesn't exist anymore but I'll tell you what it was like. It opened in Drake in seventy-six on the highway going out in the Fort Worth direction, about a mile out of town as you go up the hill, on the bend where there's the sand trap to stop the trucks coming down the hill whose brakes fail, and at first I thought it was nothing much but a kind of big gimmick to pull folk into the restaurant. Maybe that's all it was. The clever thing was it was built as a huge burger, it was shaped like a huge burger, and though close up it didn't look that impressive it was very eye-catching from a certain distance. I heard at least one fatal automobile accident occurred on that hill on account of it. You could even see it from here, looking across the other side of Drake. I don't know how it was done, it wasn't plastic, I mean when you went up and touched the sides of the burger it felt spongy, more like rubber than anything. Might've been Styrofoam or something like that. It had pieces of lettuce and tomato sticking out from the sides of the bun.

Basically it was a three-story building, with the museum on the bottom half of the burger and the restaurant on the top half and the meat in the middle. The museum was genuinely kind of fascinating. I only went once myself, just to check it out, but as I recall it had quite a lot of educational stuff on the history of burgers, who invented them and that kind of stuff. There was a section

71

about the city of Hamburg in Germany. Apparently Germans claim they invented the hamburger, German immigrants bringing it over in I don't know when, in the eighteen-somethings. I don't happen to believe that. Reason I don't comes on account of a small piece of railroad history I happen to know, which is this: in January eighteen thirty-one, January fifteen to be precise, the first six mile of railroad track for travel using steam power and carrying passengers and freight was opened in the United States. It ran out of Charleston, in South Carolina, for six mile, to a township by the name of Branchville which, as it happens, has a railroad museum nowadays called the Branchville Railroad Shrine. Year or two later the track was extended, to where? To Hamburg! And that's where the name comes from if you want my opinion, not from Hamburg in Germany. The Germans want to claim they invented the hamburger just because it happens they happen to have a city called Hamburg. Another thing is, another piece of historical baloney, is that the Russian Cossacks are meant to've invented it hundreds of years back and what they did was they'd park a slab of raw steak on their horses' backs and use it instead of a saddle to soften it up before eating it. Well big deal, who're they kidding? It's just like the Soviets, like they want to take all the credit. Anyway, if you sit on a slab of raw steak, you don't get a hamburger.

My guess is, my guess is the hamburger was originally invented by Stone Age man, but if you count Stone Age man out it was invented by the American pioneers. That was the line taken in the Burgerland museum too. They had a kind of life-size tableau of these old-timers sitting round a campfire by a wagon and eating buffalo burgers. I mean it was all fiberglass, but it was very tastefully done. They had a soundtrack with the crackling of the fire and the whinnying of the horses and also somehow they had the smell of the cooking burgers piped in. That was the smart thing, it made your mouth water. It made you hungry. But what I mean is, it's not just the invention. People in Hamburg may or may not have invented it but they didn't do much with it, did they? It's an all-American product. You can't argue against that. But it was interesting. Hiram always used to say you have to give folk one idea to carry away with them when they leave a place, and that was the one idea I took away, the burger being an American invention. This museum also had various artifacts connected to the burger, including a beautiful knife with a black horn handle that dated from the nineteenth century. It was called a burger knife. They sold replica burger knives in the souvenir store: little ones on key rings, medium-sized ones, big ones. They were priced reasonably enough, I went and bought a medium size.

The store was excellent. It was perfectly situated in the central part of the burger, the meat, between the bottom half and the top half of the bun; when I say it was perfectly situated I mean from a business point of view, I mean no one could get to the restaurant without going through the store. It was well stocked: it had burger-shaped soap, burger pendants and jewelry, little soft burgers for babies to cuddle, burger recipe books, diaries, stationery, even a fancy-dress costume where you dressed yourself up as a burger. There was a very smart board game which was called the Burgo-master where the die was burger-shaped, and as I recall it the idea was to achieve a full collection of burgers from round the world, like kangaroo burgers which I'm told they eat in Australia, and lion burgers in Africa. Things like that. I never played it but I heard about it. The best things for sale in the store, along with the burger knives, were the posters of celebrities eating burgers. I mean when you got to the restaurant there were these big black and white original photographs of celebrities eating burgers, and they weren't all B-list celebrities either. Some were quite historic, there was one photograph of President Kennedy eating a burger. Some of the photographs were personally signed. What Randy McManus had done was he'd written to all these celebrities asking if they'd be willing to be photographed for the Burgerland Experience, and it must've been a good letter because a good few of them had agreed to go along with it. I don't know what he offered them as an incentive, maybe a year's supply of hamburgers. He was the guy behind it all, Randy McManus. He was a hearty, bluff type about forty-five, who wore big pale blue pants with razor-sharp creases and had this trim little mustache, and you used to see him in town banking the proceeds, carrying this black attaché case with a little chain padlocking it to his wrists. Tell the truth, he was as pompous as hell. He liked to be called Major McManus and I think he might've served in the U.S.

military back in the days of Korea, or that was the impression he gave out.

He ran it all like a military operation, anyway. The restaurant was first-class, I'd give it at least three or four stars. They had an amazing range of burgers, not just the usual range: they had the Chiliburger and the Marlinburger, and a burger called the Drakeburger. It was a kind of cheeseburger with pepper strips laid across it and then a fried egg and sour cream on top. I had three of them, they were pretty good. Another they had was the Mao-Tse-Tungburger, which had noodles and soy sauce topping. But McManus, he had a very inventive approach to the business of pulling in the clients. He was always putting these crazy commercials on local radio, incidentally. One of these commercials started off with the sound of someone trying to blow into a trumpet but not being able to succeed; all you could hear was this kind of strained blowing noise and then a voice said something like: "This guy is trying to blow into a trumpet, but there's one of McManus' Drakeburgers up the spout." And that was it. There was another one of a guy trying to crack a joke but you can't hear a word, and the voice says: "This guy is trying to crack a joke, but he's eating a McManus' Drakeburger at the same time." It was like a punchline. They were always like that. There was another one of a guy trying to kiss his wife while she was eating a Drakeburger. He was saying, "C'mon honey, give us a kiss . . . c'mon honey" and she was going "Oaaaah . . . " and the voice said: "He'd like to kiss her but she'd sooner eat a Drakeburger." I know it doesn't sound that funny telling it now, but it had a kind of weird crazy quality that was somehow different. I wish I could play one of them to you. They weren't like normal commercials, they were kind of collectors' items. Randy McManus was like that, although as I say he didn't look like it, in these sky-blue pants. But he was smart. One time, it must've been in nineteen seventy-nine, he held a Burger Parade, from downtown Drake up the hill to the museum, and everyone who took part was given free burgers. Hundreds showed up. Then another time he held a burger-eating contest and I would've taken part but for the fact it was just when I'd gone and busted my ankle, so I had to miss out. It was pretty disappointing, especially when I heard the winner'd only eaten seven burgers in the ten minutes, which I knew I could've beaten pretty easily.

But the Burgerland Experience did pretty well. It made quite a name for itself, for a time it was getting forty thousand visitors a year, if not more. I could see it across the valley, lit up at night like a beacon for all America, and it got me thinking, it encouraged me in what I was doing, it gave me a certain faith. Being an American I have that faith bred into me but even so it was an encouragement. It wasn't just the Burgerland Experience; at the time, plenty of other museums were cropping up all over Texas. In Tyler there was a Waffle Museum, for example, still is. Constant had one on the history of cotton, and I've heard of more than one peanut museum. Somewhere in Arkansas according to Hiram there is, or was, a Concentration Camp

Experience. It's a recreation of the concentration camps in World War Two Europe, with watchtowers and barbed wire and accommodation blocks and guards in German uniform and prisoners. The prisoners are trying to tunnel out beyond the barbed wire under the eyes of the guards and when they escape, which is every afternoon dead on three o'clock, big crowds turn up to cheer them on. Like a kind of community event. Members of the public can volunteer to become a guard by paying a few extra dollars, if they like. Most of the prisoners are gunned down, shot in the back by the guards. I'm not sure if they've got a gas chamber or anything like that, for gassing the Jews; I guess you wouldn't get too many volunteers for that, though there's a big public appetite for all kinds of experience. What I'm saying is it's a sizeable industry nowadays. Hiram called it home-grown tourism, and I reckon one way of seeing it is as a kind of local crop. You till the soil, you sow the seed, you reap whatever you reap. Sure, some seed falls on stony ground, but some seed falls on fertile ground and you get a crop at the end off of it. That's the way, that's what Americans have always done so successfully.

Of course, you need to find something no one else is doing. No one else was offering the Fattest Man in America, by definition. Well, that first year of Saturdays we had a total of seven hundred and fifty-five visitors, almost all from the Drake area, and the following year, when I opened full-time, we had more than five thousand.

By then I'd taken down the notice about touching. People who wanted to touch had to pay extra, like being a prison guard in the Concentration Camp Experience. Many people did pay, most people. I had a rope barrier put up round my body, and a security guard on hand to intervene immediately should anyone overstep the mark. Sometimes I had two security guards. They were recruited by Hiram. They wore dark suits and white shirts and black ties. Then we had the catering manager, and a ticketing supervisor, and waitresses. I had them dressed in the black skirts and white frilly aprons like the maids at the Ranelagh Grand, the waitresses. I always insisted on the staff being smart and courteous. Smartness, courtesy, and respect, those were things again I took from my experiences at the Ranelagh Grand. Not that I was a Leonard Saker. I always tried treating the staff with the same respect that I expected them to accord me. That's the only way. It's worth remembering, a happy employee is always going to be a more efficient and hard-working employee. That's one of the maxims I'll be putting in my business manual.

Getting on to Hiram. Hiram Cutler was my business manager. A short, lively man with sharp eyes. My promoter, if you like.

It was Hiram who contacted me. He wrote me a letter in which he offered assistance in exploiting my business potential. He proposed an initial meeting, no fee, no strings attached. I still have the letter. Embossed in purple with the head of the American bald eagle and three Latin words, *Veritas, Fidelitas, Virtutas*, which roughly translates as Truth, Faithfulness, and Virtue, very courteous and very open. It introduced him as a business consultant, with a degree from Cornell and qualifications in accountancy and business management. It explained that if, after a meeting, I wished to take advantage of his services, I could do so; if not, that was my decision.

Maybe I wasn't cautious enough, maybe I ought've been more suspicious, but if you go through life suspicious of everything, you don't get anywhere. And an opportunity unexplored is an opportunity wasted. That's another useful maxim. I reckoned I had nothing to lose, I might as well find out what he had to say. So I invited him round.

I liked the look of him from the start. He was brisk, early thirties, smart in appearance and bristling with energy. He pointed out that I was seriously underutilizing my assets. I said how I'd been described as unique.

"Sure! We live in a mass-production age, and you are a unique product. You are a phenomenon. There is nothing like you in the whole of the United States. How widely are you known?"

"Folk in Drake know me," I said.

"Sure! Sure! People in Drake know of you all right. But Michael—once you get beyond Drake, who's ever heard of you? No one. No one at all. You don't have any name recognition." He spread his arms. "There's a whole world out there, waiting! They need to hear from you! At the moment, no one's hearing a chirrup. For most of America, you don't even exist!"

In a few minutes, talking at a lick, he sketched out a dozen or more ideas to help develop the business. Proper advertising. Approaches to the media. Better facilities for visitors, including a big parking lot. A store (he called it an emporium) selling souvenirs and tailor-made merchandise. I should see myself, he said, as a great entertainer, as a professional showman; I was putting on a show and it needed to have some magic to it.

"You're the star, Michael," he said. "That's what your job is, being the star. And you have to preserve your star status. You have to build up an aura. If you take calls on the telephone, if you get involved in the day-to-day operations, you detract from that star quality. You become an ordinary person. Who wants to pay good money to see an ordinary person? No one. So what you need is a manager. A drudge. Someone who can run the operation."

When I heard that, I suddenly saw the future. I saw how it might develop; I knew I was going to become famous.

"I've got my ma," I said.

"Is she professionally qualified?" he asked.

I admitted that she wasn't.

"Look," he said, "your mother is your mother. She's your mother. That's her business, being a mother. But she's not a manager. A mother's not a manager. If you want to have a manager, if you want to see your business *grow*, you need a proper manager. That's someone who you can hire, *and* who you can fire. You can't fire your father. You can't fire your mother. It's a different relationship, Michael."

"That's true," I said. And then I must have hesitated, because he went on: "Michael, I always find it best to be totally candid with clients. Is that acceptable to you?"

"Sure," I said. "Pitch in."

"Any professional who looks at your business as it now stands would know, without having to be told, that you do not have a manager. The operation displays all the characteristics. For a start, there's no restroom. If someone comes to see you wants to visit the restroom, what do they do? They visit your private bathroom. That's not good. If they want to buy a souvenir for the kids, they can't. They go away disappointed. That's not good either. Your whole strategy is one of zero management; in fact it's not a strategy at all. Any professional'd be saying to you what I'm saying to you. Having your mother managing, and I put that in inverted commas"—he indicated, as such with his fingers—"is not a help. It's a hindrance. Now, that's fine if you don't mind your business gradually plateauing out. Because, okay, at the moment, yearly, you have five thousand people from Drake coming to view you. What happens when the whole of Drake has seen you? What then? It's a limited market. If you want to survive, you have to expand, that's a business fundamental."

Now it wasn't strictly true that everyone came from Drake. I'd had folks from Motson and Paris and Constant, and even a few from Tyler and Fort Worth. But I could see what he said made sense. You see, by this time, the Burgerland Experience'd closed down, and here's why. Randy McManus had taken the profits and quit. He'd sold up and passed it on to some other guy who didn't have the same flair or know-how or ingenuity, and it'd gone bust. Simple as that, took about eight month, that was it. Finish. And the place was dismantled. Well, I didn't want that to happen to me, and so there and then I offered Hiram the post of business manager. To his great credit, he refused to accept immediately. No, he said, I should reflect on his words for longer and then, if I still felt sure in my own mind, contact him again.

"The one thing that I will say to you, Michael," he said—in those days he called me Michael, it was only later on he changed to Mickey—"is that this should be your decision and yours alone. Not your mother's, not anybody else's. This is you. It's your future. I'm not trying to persuade you one way or the other. Chew it over. Only other thing, Michael," he said before he left, "is this. The future's not tomorrow. It's never tomorrow. It's now. You need to grab it while it's here."

These remarks made a big impression on me. I can't hardly express how big, except by recalling how, after Hiram Cutler'd left, I was in a kind of daze. I couldn't stay still; I wandered outside, still clutching his business card, and lay in the shade of a palm. There was this fighter airplane high in the skies. At first it was big and heavy, but as it traveled on it grew tinier and tinier till it was just a speck of fire in the western firmament. I watched it but I wasn't really watching. My brain was whirling with excitement. I saw my name going round the world. I saw the magazines, the photographs, the cameras, the people, the money, the lot. It was a kind of vision, I guess, like seeing the Blue Falls for the first time.

I'll tell you about the Blue Falls, in case you don't know. Not everyone's heard of them, even in Drake, they're a kind of secret round here, I guess. A state secret. That's because they're not on the highway. You can't drive up to the Blue Falls like you're driving up to the local drugstore or movie center.

That is to say, you can drive about thirty mile out of Drake in the Constant direction and you get to the settlement Blue Falls. Nothing much to it. Diner, gas station, a motel that probably hasn't even got a single star to its name. A minute and you're through, blink and you've missed it. No; for the Falls themselves, you have to drive on a couple of mile until on your left, to the north, you can see this kind of craggy ridge. A bluff, you might call it. In front there's rough scrubby ground, a few trees and bushes of the thorny kind, with a dirt track leading off. And you can see the railroad between you and the bluff.

We sometimes used to go along the railroad coming from Constant, and my pa or ma would always point excitedly and say, "Over there, see. There're the Blue Falls." I never could see anything, not with the train bumping along. The windows of the car were always dusty and dirty, or so it seemed, but even if they'd been clean I wouldn't't've seen much.

One summer day we drove there. I seem to recall we didn't have our own car but that my pa had the loan of Uncle Bobby's pickup, and when we all squeezed in it being so heavy the bumper was hitting the ground, and my ma said she'd stick at home. As I said, she's no walker, she's never held with exercise too much. Even so, we scraped the road all the way, and I guess Uncle Bobby mayn't have been too happy when he got it back.

We parked by the dirt track and set off walking. We were camping. I mean, camping. My pa always liked camping, he'd say it made him feel like one of the early pioneers, sleeping under the stars. He liked the pioneer spirit. He used to say, when he saw a trail, that's an old buffalo trail. He liked to think of the buffalos, roaming the prairies.

Hilary and Zoe were there too. I can't have been so fat, but I'd have been fat all the same. I'd say I was no more'n nine or ten.

So we walk, and walk, and walk some more. This is how I recall it, anyway. We walk and walk along the dirt track, but after we cross the railroad there's no proper trail, just little half trails that turn into quarter trails and then stop altogether in clumps of thorn trees. Or there was a trail and we lost it, I guess. It was summer, and the sun was grilling, and I got tired soon enough. Pa kept on telling us that it'd be worth it when we got there, and that it wasn't much farther. He'd point and say, "See the bluff. See the trees. It's just over there." Whatever he was pointing at never seemed to get much closer, though, he was kidding us along.

The trail up the side of the bluff was thin and crumbling. I was at the back of the line, I know, and bits of stone kept bouncing down that'd been dislodged by Hilary and Zoe and Pa. And I was very tired, too. I guess that's why, when I heard it, when I got on to the ridge, I didn't realize what I was hearing. Just a dull roar, like an airplane a few seconds after it's gone over. Then I came over the top of the bluff and the others were waiting, and we went on to the river, above the falls.

The river is wide at that point, a great body of water. As it approached the lip of the falls it was so smooth it was like moving glass. You could see the clouds and trees in it. It was flowing down such a gentle slope you could nearly believe it wasn't flowing at all. It went over the lip, still smooth as ever, and so slow, weightless, like a dream. What happened then, nothing showed, except a few wisps of spray, but you could hear the boom of the water far below.

We walked down to the lip and looked over the drop. The water was still slowly falling, plunging toward the gorge with its jagged black rocks, from which rose these great clouds of spray. The sun shone through them, creating a multitude of rainbows. So there were two movements in opposition to each other, the falling water and in front of that the rising spray. It was kind of mesmeric, I couldn't take it in. My eyes kept on following the water down until it struck the bottom, and then following the spray up and up, as far as the lip, at which point they latched onto another section of falling water. Or I watched the water foaming down the narrow black gorge.

Why was it so grand? I guess you'd have to mention the incredible contrast between the glassy stillness before the lip, and what followed. Then the sense of power. That was humbling. The roar was so loud it shut out everything else, it was a total experience. I've heard of the sunrise down on the Grand Canyon, but this was pretty good too.

That night we camped, down by the gorge. We lit a fire and cooked food, and sang campfire songs. "Yankee Doodle Dandy," "Camptown Races," "Daisy Bell." My pa had a tin whistle he played, and our faces were dappled by the firelight. The stars came out too. And the falls roared and seethed below us. "It never stops," said Pa. "It never stops. The falls'll be here till the end of time, till they're switch off by God."

I felt like one of the first Americans that night. I felt a true pioneer, alone in the wilderness.

The next morning Zoe and I walked back up to the top of the falls, and we got a big dead branch from a tree and swung it into the water. This was maybe several hundred yards above the falls. The branch was quickly caught by the power of the current and was borne along toward the lip. The head of the branch stuck up like the antlers of a big stag, and as it sailed along I thought how it had no knowledge of what lay in store for it. It wasn't exactly that I thought it was conscious, but that I felt myself in the position of the branch—sailing along, smooth as you like. When it reached the lip it seemed to hang there for a long moment before tilting forward and tipping into the gorge.

I've never been back. I couldn't go back now, being so fat, walk all that way . . . shit, it's as much as I can do now to move much of a distance at all. My legs won't support me. But I'm not certain I'd want to go back, even if I could. You can't go back to the past. Still, I often think of Pa's remark about it never stopping. All these years, the water not stopping, never stopping. Even now, every second, on and on and on. And how, at the end of time, after God switches it all off, it'll be frozen in an instant, all that water—the river like ice, the falls hanging in midair like a frozen curtain.

When the water was falling it seemed to have a kind of blue tinge to it; that's why they're called the Blue Falls, I guess.

3

Business. How does one make a business successful? What's the magic formula? It's a question that has preoccupied the greatest minds in human history, from ancient times to the present. Thing is, and folk don't always appreciate this, there is no magic formula. What works in one place at one time may not work in another place at another time. Having said which, you have to also say that certain basic precepts need to be adhered to for a venture to stand any chance of success in a competitive business world. Putting this another way, as my pa might've put it: doesn't matter how nicely carved a chair may be, if it's only got one leg, it won't stand up.

There's the conception, and then there's execution of that conception. Before meeting Hiram I had the right conception, but I couldn't execute it. He knew about execution. I'm not saying he was a business genius, but he was trained, or at least he said he was trained and'd been to Cornell and I had no reason to doubt him, not at that juncture. Things may not have turned out exactly as I envisaged, but I still believe the decision to hire Hiram to be the most important of what I describe as my fledgling business career.

Over the next year, as a result of the changes that we introduced, audience figures began to rise and rise. The year before Hiram, as I said, five thousand people came to view me; in the year that followed, eleven thousand two hundred; the year after that, thirty-three thousand nine hundred. Those are the attendance figures. Our takings, however, accelerated at a much greater velocity, with ticket prices more than tripling. As Hiram pointed out, if you don't charge a reasonable admission charge, people won't feel they're getting anything much worth having.

Let me list a few of our achievements in those three years.

First, a major program of building works. We built a cafeteria, an exhibition area, restrooms, emporium, and parking lot. Outside the house we erected a fluorescent sign, ninety feet high; you can still see the concrete base out there now. It read: THE FATTEST MAN IN AMERICA, and every three seconds, day and night, it changed color. The sequence ran: purple, green, red, yellow, gold. It could be seen from much of Drake, and I reckon, from what folk told me, it became the town's best-known landmark.

Second, promotion. On the basis of market research, we ran an extensive campaign to raise public awareness of the business outside Drake. We ran regular commercials on local radio stations. We had tie-ins with the food industry.

Within a radius of a hundred mile we had billboards outside every airport. We sponsored certain events, especially those related to food; we encouraged friendly forms of journalism, especially in women's magazines. We targeted women's magazines. "Nothing you have ever seen, or heard, or read, nothing you are ever likely to see, or hear, or read, can prepare you for the sight of this phenomenon known as Mickey." That's what one article said. Joke is, it was word for word what Hiram wrote himself. We mailed out the publicity and these jerks of journalists were too lazy to write their own copy!

So what did a visitor get? What did he or she see?

It was like this:

On arrival, people first bought their tickets. There were different types of tickets. We charged seven dollars per person for straight viewing without photography, twelve, for viewing with photography; twenty, if they wanted to touch. Twenty got them photography as well. Kids, students, and graybeards half price. I reckon it was good value. Logic tells me that, if the charges were too high, we would have seen a fall in numbers, whereas the reverse was true. At busy periods, lines sometimes formed at the ticket booths.

Visitors then passed into the exhibition area, which presented a pictorial history of fatness. History down the ages, from prehistoric times to the present. Yes sir! Drawings, photographs, models. Fat Greeks, fat Romans, fat Egyptians. A certain amount of physiological data, but presented in a lively and fun way. What is the purpose of fat? Is mankind getting fatter? It was educational. I was proud of it. We also put in distorted mirrors, distorting mirrors I mean, which progressively fattened and shortened the onlooker. The idea was, this was Hiram's idea, that folk'd seem fatter as they moved toward me, and then thinner as they left.

So the viewing was the next stage, that was when they saw me, took their photographs, whatever. I'll be saying more about that in a minute. After the viewing came the emporium. Jewelry, trinkets, models in porcelain and chocolate, a Mickey bathroom scale, Mickey notepaper, Mickey cuddly toys, Mickey tea towels, postcards, posters. One of the posters was life-size. It was a very tasteful patriotic image. I was reclining on some beanbags, with the Stars and Stripes draped across my waist. It sold very well indeed, both framed and unframed. But we had a very wide range of products, including an inflatable Mickey plastic boat for young kiddies to use in wading pools and the like.

One of our best-selling products was a video of me stroking Tiger, my cat. It lasted about ten minutes. We packaged it nicely, we dressed it up in a plastic gold cover. In one year we sold more than fifty thousand copies. In one year!

I had two cats in those days. One was Tiger, the other Lincoln, after Abraham Lincoln. Lincoln's still with me. He's black and has gold eyes, and he's a good hunter. He goes off at nighttime and brings back his latest prey, like a dead bird. Drops it in my hand. I guess he reckons I'm a big cat, and a dead bird is a kind of tribute. Tiger was different, very home-loving and domestic. He liked company. He loved being stroked, he used to purr real loud. Only thing was, if you stopped stroking and he wanted you to go on, he'd sometimes dig his claws into you. He was a Persian cat, with long white hair and sleepy green eyes.

I put the video on this morning, in preparation for making this recording, and it made me weep—just seeing him again. I hadn't watched it in so long. There's not much happens in it. He comes up and rubs the side of his body against the wall of my belly, then my hand reaches out and tickles him behind his ears and under his chin. Then you can see him arching his back, and purring, and suddenly he starts licking my belly with his tongue. He goes on, licking and licking, moving from one spot to another, which was something he liked doing. Maybe the saltiness of the skin, I don't know. He was an affectionate cat. After a time he settles down and washes his front paws and falls asleep. That's all. There's no word spoken, and you never see my face or anything, but it's kind of quiet and meditative, and I've spoken to folk who've said that watching it brought them a kind of inner tranquillity at times of stress.

The cafeteria followed. Nothing very special, but it served up good American food. Buns, bagels, pastries, pizzas, cookies. Buy three cookies, get one free. Free Mickey balloons for all kids.

One consequence of these changes was that Ma no

longer lived with me. She and Hiram didn't see eye to eye and she moved back to Constant. I was sorry about that. I could see that it was necessary for the business to have a professional manager, obviously. Hiram was right, having your mother as a manager was crazy. I didn't want her to go and I offered her a job running the cafeteria but she wouldn't have any of it: she packed her bags and quit. And after that we weren't in contact for a long time, even at Thanksgiving. It upset me, of course it upset me. At first, to be truthful, after she'd gone, I felt kind of relieved, but your ma's your ma, and we'd always been close, especially after Pa passed on, and as time went by I used to miss her. I asked Hiram to mail her a copy of the video with Tiger as a kind of peace offering, and I waited for her reply, but it never came. Day after day I waited for a letter or something but it never came. Hiram said I should take it easy and relax, but I couldn't help feeling a certain bitterness, and I hardened my heart against my own mother. Only quite recently I discovered Hiram'd never sent her the video, just as he never did plenty of things he was meant to do.

I'm not putting all the blame on Hiram, however. I guess I should've managed things better.

The most important part of "The Fattest Man in America" for the visitors was when they set eyes on me for the first time. The seminal moment, Hiram said. He and I spent many long hours refining and refining that experience in order to make it as satisfying as possible, because we really did want folk to feel they'd got their money's worth. We wanted to make it perfect, and I reckon we got it pretty close to perfection. Not absolute perfection, but pretty darn close.

Early on I made a decision that I would keep my bedroom private, and that the viewing would take place in the living room. We didn't call it the living room any longer, we called it the Shrine. That was my idea, after the Branchville Railroad Shrine. I always liked the idea of a shrine, it made it seem special. It just had that kind of ring to it made folk sit up and take notice.

Well, what happened was this: I'd be lying on my bean-bags, generally on my side, either presenting my back or my front. Certain details changed over the three years, but at the start I was wearing mirror dark glasses and very baggy short pants. The pants were Stars and Stripes pants, to emphasize my patriotism. The blinds, which were wooden, were kept shut, and the general ambient light in the room was low dark red, to provide an air of . . . an area of . . . an aura of mystery. A single spotlight shone on the beanbags not from directly above but from the wall opposite, so that while parts of my body were brightly illuminated, other parts were left in shadow. Behind the beanbags, there was this large mirror, so I looked twice the size I was. It was carefully done.

Beside the beanbags I had a supply of food, usually cookies and corn, not to eat but for the general ambience. I never liked anyone to watch me eating. I had water too, because I often used to get thirsty. A security guard was always in attendance. The responsibility of the security

94

guards was to check that no one came too close or took photographs, unless they had the appropriate tickets, and to ensure a speedy throughput. It was all worked out. Three minutes was the usual viewing period, but at especially busy times of years, in the school vacations, we cut that to two and a half.

Viewing times were from ten to one, and two to five. Six hours a day; it's a long time, you try it. What did I do all this time, as I lay on my beanbags, as the visitors filed through and looked at me? Well, I generally had Tiger with me, and I used to stroke him. And I read, some of the time, I read. I read fiction. John Steinbeck books; he's my favorite American writer. *Of Mice and Men*, that's my favorite. *The Grapes of Wrath*, that's another.

Another thing I used to do is listen to country music, on headphones. That was the first thing me and Hiram didn't agree on. Country music's my taste, it's what I like; I've always liked it, ever since I can remember. My pa used to like it, too. One of the programs he always made a point of listening in to was Constant County Radio's "Country Hour", every evening at seven. You can get it in Drake and I still listen to it now, I was listening a few moments back. The D.J.s are very knowledgeable, especially a D.J. by the name of Teddy Montezuma. You learn a lot, it's pretty educational. I'd recommend it to anyone.

Hiram didn't know a thing about country, he didn't even call it country. When he talked about country music he never called it country, he always called it hillbilly—in a kind of derogatory way. Another phrase he used was hick music. I tried explaining to him how there's lots of different types of country music, because not everybody appreciates that—I mean there's cowboy country music, the kind of music sung by the Sons of the Pioneers and there's Western swing, and then there's the kind of Jim Reeves sound, I don't know what to call that—country croonin', maybe. And bluegrass. What I like about country is that it's relaxed and very easy, comfortable, restful, relaxed American music, but it's also about really painful emotional subjects. It's about despair and falling in and out of love and—I mean it's very heartfelt. Hiram never said he didn't like country, he wasn't that stupid. What he just said was he didn't reckon it was appropriate, not to a show that was meant to be high art. He wanted religious music, spiritual music. Monks chanting, that kind of thing. If it was a Shrine, he said, it had to have religious music.

We had quite a discussion about it. Several discussions, tell the truth. He'd say, he was just thinking from a business point of view, what would work, and I'd say, look, I'm the one who has to listen to it, which I reckon was a valid point. I'd've gone nuts listening to monks all day. So we found a compromise. I listened to country on headphones, and we had the monks chanting in the background for the visitors. Not just Christian monks. Sometimes Buddhist monks, lamas, you know?

I respected Hiram's judgment on these matters. He had a genius for hitting the right note.

What I never did was talk. I reckon, looking back, that

was the single most significant change that Hiram and I introduced, not talking. Silence. But not just not talking, also not relating in any personal way to the viewers. The relationship was designed to be simple, subject and object, spectactor and spectated, that was the beauty of it. I didn't even move very often, I tried not to move at all. What I offered was a tableau, a picture, a piece of art which was also real life. If you follow me. The Fat Man in the Shrine.

It was funny. Often they'd try to make me react. They'd call out: "Hey! There! Michael! Mickey! Ya hear me? How ya doin'! Howsa weight?" Questions like that. Or they'd try to make me laugh, pulling faces or cracking stupid one-line wisecracks. Or shouting insults. The kids used to do that sometimes. They'd say: "If I put a pin in him, d'ya figure he'll pop?" They'd say: "Where's the valve?" I got wise to it all, it didn't faze me one little bit. I'd had it at high school, after all. If I happened to be listening on headphones, besides, I couldn't hear a word they were saying.

I mean there were lots of reactions. Sometimes people used to burst into hysterical laughter, or just ordinary laughter, especially if my belly was making a lot of noise. I've remembered that medical term I was telling you about earlier, incidentally, for the sounds of the belly. Borborygmus. Borborygmus. I was told that by Dr. Coughlan, who is my present doctor. There're medical terms for almost anything, I guess. And if I had an attack of the borborygmus, people'd sometimes laugh. Most were respectful, however. Reverential even. It was their first reactions that I used to love, when they first came into

97

the Shrine, and realized what they were looking at. That "Wow!" and their hands going to their mouths in shock.

It's hard to explain, really. I wouldn't say I'm an exhibitionist by nature, I'm quite shy, and in the early days the personal nature of the comments did rile me occasionally. Same as when I was a boy, I hated people looking at me on account of my fatness. What it was, I guess, was hating being different. All children are like that, they want to be like everyone else. Only as you grow to manhood you understand that's not possible, everyone's different to everyone else, we all have our own talents given us by Providence that we must do our utmost to use to the fullest.

Therefore, as time went on, I accepted my role as a showman. When people showed pleasure, it gave me real pleasure; I watched them from behind my dark glasses, if I wasn't reading or thinking, and felt a glow. However, as I say, I didn't ever show it, I just glowed within. The essence of my performance, as Hiram used to say to me, lay in my passivity. Inertness was the key. You could say, I guess, that the essence lay in my existence.

Sometimes folk from Constant would show up. People I used to know. Kids from the school who used to call me the Earthquake, or shout names at me. "Fat boy! Fat boy! Fat! Look at his tits!" Or, when I used to try to run, they'd shout "Keep on losing, fattie." Now here they were, with their made-up wives and rackety little children, paying good American dollars for a little glimpse of me, and I half felt like saying: "Who's losing now? Hey?" But I didn't. I didn't react, I kept quiet. I got pretty good at not reacting.

One of the teachers from Constant High showed up once. He taught science, taught me about the discovery of gravity by Sir Isaac Newton, in England, U.K. That story about Sir Isaac sitting in the orchard and the apple drops on his head.

Funny thing about that story, I always pictured it as the same apple tree as the one in the Garden of Eden. The Tree of Knowledge of Good and Evil. The apple that hit Sir Isaac being from the same tree as the apple that Eve bit into.

It's a dumb idea, I know, as there's nothing exactly good nor evil about gravity. Gravity is as gravity is. But I like the notion that what hit Sir Isaac on the head was a lump of knowledge.

I'd like to know why no one before Sir Isaac cottoned on to the existence of gravity. No one thought, why don't we float off? Didn't cross anyone's mind. Then Sir Isaac sits himself down in the orchard and, bang, it hits him on the head.

That's often the story of success in business. Takes one smart idea and it's all you need. Like Thomas Edison thinking up the lightbulb, and then having another great idea, the idea of the movies. You could say that Thomas Edison, he was hit on the head by two apples.

Edison got rich. I don't know about Newton, I guess it wasn't easy to market gravity.

Where was I? Okay—

This teacher who showed up was called Mr. Matthews,

he was a pleasant enough guy. He had a sense of humor, unlike some of the other teachers, who were mostly dumb. He also tried to stop the kids from teasing me, which I was grateful for. I recognized him at once. He was wearing the same old check shirt and jacket and beige trousers he always did, but I noticed his socks were mismatched. With him there was a woman, I guess his wife, who was quite pretty, and also this little handicapped boy, who must've been their son. Mentally or physically handicapped, I don't rightly know, but his face was kind of on one side and he couldn't control his lips and when he walked his ankles seemed to roll over. He couldn't keep still, the boy. Mrs. Matthews had a tight hold on his wrist but he kept on writhing like he was struggling to get away.

Mr. Matthews stopped and he said to me, "Hullo Michael." He always called me Michael, not Mickey. I was never Mickey till Hiram made me Mickey. "You won't remember me."

As I say, I don't usually say anything, but I'd always liked Mr. Matthews and I didn't want to seem too rude, so I took off my dark glasses and said: "Hullo, Mr. Matthews. Of course I remember you."

I held out a hand and we shook hands.

"How are you?" he said.

"I'm fine," I said. "I'm in good shape."

"How heavy are you now?"

"Some way over eight hundred seventy."

"Really!" He was plainly impressed. "I do hope you won't get much heavier."

100

"It's not my decision," I said. "I eat normally, and if I get heavier I get heavier."

"Right," he said. He seemed at a loss. "I wasn't sure if it would be you here. We were just driving along the freeway, and we saw the sign. But you're enjoying yourself, are you?"

"I'm doing fine," I said. "Are you still teaching at Constant?"

"I am," he said. "I'm probably stuck there now, unfortunately, for the duration. By the way, we enjoyed the mirrors," he said. "Very amusing."

That was in relation to the distorted mirrors, the ones I've got here now. We had them in the exhibition area. Anyway, he said how much he enjoyed the mirrors and I thanked him. Then he introduced me to his wife. He said to her: "It's always fascinating seeing what happens to pupils. Sometimes you can predict what'll happen, other times they do something completely unexpected."

We had quite a conversation. He asked about various other boys and girls at high school who were in my class, but I couldn't tell him anything much. I guess it must be hard teaching, watching these pupils you've striven to knock something into their skulls going off into the unknown each year to make their fortunes and leaving you behind like you're unwanted living off a teacher's salary. Like a snake shedding its skin. I also felt sorry for him on account of the boy. I reckon he was age seven or eight, but it wasn't that easy to tell; afterwards, I thought he might've been much older. Strangest thing, all the time

101

we were talking, the boy was rolling his eyes at me, and then as Mr. Matthews began taking some photographs of me the boy suddenly laughed very loudly, in a kind of hysterical way that was almost frightening, and when they tried to make him stop laughing, Mr. and Mrs. Matthews, he got even louder. I don't know what he was laughing at, but he was nearly screaming. In the end they just had to hustle him out, holding him by each elbow, like he was a prisoner or something. It was kind of scary, and pretty sad, to be honest. Providence had dealt him a bad deal. At least he was American. To be like that almost anywhere else in the world would be pretty terrible, I reckon.

I had one of the Mickey posters mailed to the boy, signed, with my compliments, for him to stick up on his bedroom wall. I didn't know the address, so I got it sent to the school. Mr. Matthews wrote back to thank me, a very pleasant letter. I haven't heard from him since, but I guess he's still teaching away.

★

I've just listened back on the tape and there's some more I want to add in relation to my ma. It was the robe that really made her leave. She'd made this velvet robe, did I tell you? She's a very good seamstress and she made this beautiful purple velvet robe with gold braid that fastened round the neck, and a cord tie. I looked good in it, too, but Hiram said it masked my fatness. When I wore it, people couldn't see how truly fat I was. Also, he said, the robe made me look like an Arab sheikh. It was his idea to put me in the Stars and Stripes pants. Ma didn't like them, she hated them, she said they looked stupid. I guess Hiram was right from the business perspective, he knew what worked and what didn't work, but I can see it from Ma's perspective.

"I don't like this man," she said. "He's got you trussed up like a darn chicken."

I explained to her. "Hiram's a businessman. He's got business acumen. He's got a qualification in business management from Cornell."

"So he says," she sniffed. "I don't like his eyes. He's got dead eyes."

"You can't condemn a man on account of his eyes, Ma."

"I can do what I like, thank you," she said. Then she said, in a voice of doom: "The eyes are the windows to the soul, your granpa always said. The eyes are the windows to the soul. That man ain't got no soul, far as I can tell."

And a few days later, out she went, back to Constant, even though I offered her the post of manageress of the cafeteria.

That's my ma for you. She's always been a stubborn type of person, but she's got a heart of gold. I'm not just saying that on account of her being my mother, either, I mean she has.

What else should I tell you? I used to get people from far-off places. Canada, Brazil, Chile, China, Europe, you

103

name it. The word spread. It was crazy. Some of the visitors used to write to me, I'd get more than thirty letters a day, on average. I mean the letters still arrive even now, occasionally. Me and Martha, we laugh at them. There was this one, I've got it for you, typical enough, from a woman who lives in London, England. She wrote, and I quote:

Dear Mickey,
I am a 74-year-old grandmother. I've lived a long life, and travelled widely. I've been to Australia, where I have seen Ayers Rock and the Sydney Opera House and the Barrier Reef. I have also been to southern Africa, both to visit the safari and Victoria Falls. And yet I have never had an experience like the one which you provide. To see you in the flesh was truly spectacular, believe me, a revelation, a highlight not only of my trip to the United States but of my entire life. The memory continues to inspire me in my daily life here in London—

"Inspiring" is one word that folk often deployed in their letters; "inspiring" or "life-affirming." I once had a cute little postcard from an Italian man. His message ended: "Only in America! Keep eating!"

I also received letters from people who had not visited me here in Drake, but had heard of me through articles in magazines. Fat people, especially. I guess they looked on me as a role model, because I wasn't ashamed of being fat. I've never been ashamed, not at all, on the contrary:

I was determined to glorify the fact of my fatness. I wanted to celebrate it.

I also received letters from schoolchildren. We had parties of schoolchildren round quite often, although the authorities didn't like it. Not sufficiently educational. I say, if it's not educational seeing a man of eight hundred plus pound in the flesh, the fattest man in America, a piece of living history, what is? Why is it less educational than visiting the Grand Canyon? What's the problem? The attitude of the state authorities was quite negative and anti-fat, to be frank and honest. I mean some of the letters I received! But I reckon most people who took the trouble to visit were satisfied with what they saw, in fact more than satisfied. They'd never seen anything like me before, and probably never would again, unless they came back to a second viewing.

In fact, as it happens, our consumer research showed that many people did return two or three times. Chiefly women, and that suggests there was a kind of erotic element to my appeal, though as I've said before I reckon the main appeal just lay in the flesh. Okay, not just the flesh, but also the fame. I was to be the fattest man in America, maybe the fattest man in the world, and that must have counted for something. Mustn't it? I was making a good deal of money, too, and being rich is meant to have its attractions. That's one of the things about fatness, incidentally. Generally speaking, the fat aren't rich, the fat aren't rich or famous, it's a thin man's world. From that perspective I was bucking the trend.

As the business built up I could've spent my entire

waking life doing interviews with journalists, but I never enjoyed interviews. The journalists'd always ask the same lousy questions, like they were clones of each other. I'd be half asleep with boredom, mostly, and they'd be asking what I ate, and how much I ate, and what was my favorite food (steak) and my favorite writer (John Steinbeck) and my favorite singers (Glen Campbell and Johnny Cash), and when I last took exercise, and when I first got fat, and what I considered the disadvantages were of being fat.

D'you regret being fat, given the disadvantages?

It's a lousy question; of course I don't regret it. I'd say to that, one man's disadvantage is another man's advantage.

D'you enjoy being fat?

Now, enjoyment. Enjoyment. What's enjoyment? I'd answer that I enjoy being me. I happen to be fat. Providence made me fat.

They'd ask whether I'd considered medical treatment to remove my fat. Suck it out or something. Leave me like a shriveled prune.

"No sir," I say, "thanking you for your kind suggestion. I prefer staying the way God made me."

They'd ask if I reckoned I was going to go on getting fatter.

"Well sir, I don't reckon that's up to me. If God wants to make me fatter, sure He'll make me fatter. If He wants to slim me down He'll slim me down."

Are you a strong believer in God?

"Look," I'd say, "tell you this, write it down: I believe

God's an American. I believe He's in possession of an American passport."

How d'you see yourself?

"Me? I see myself as a pioneer, an American pioneer."

The most difficult question was: "What's it like being so fat? What's it feel like?"

That's also the most interesting question, the only interesting question. What's it like being like what you are? I couldn't ever answer that. Like you can't turn back the clock, you can't become someone else. But I worked out an answer. What I'd say is: "*My brain's not fat. My brain's the same size as other people's.*"

That's what I'd say. They didn't want me to say that, of course, they'd look disappointed. Scribbling in their little notepads.

They'd never pay much attention to my answers, the journalists. They knew what they wanted to write and they were going to write it whatever I said. The English were the most difficult. In England they talk about weight in stone, so when I'd say eight hundred pound they'd say how many stone is that, and I'd say it depends on the size of your stone. I don't mind that but I did object to their tone. Do you ever feel guilty about your food consumption? I couldn't take that, why the heck should I feel guilty? It was the way the English journalists put their questions that really riled me. Slightly superior, their noses in the air. La-di-da. I know what it is with the English. Back in history they had an Empire and they lost it, and now they can't accept the fact that America's the greatest nation on earth. Twice this century America's had to go bail them out of a war they were losing. I'm sorry for them. But the French aren't much better. When I told them God was an American, that always riled them.

What I'm trying to express is there's not enough respect. I was raised by my ma and pa to believe you should respect people for what they are, and I've always tried to act on that basis in my private and public lives. But some journalists were just deliberately disrespectful. I gave an interview to a Swedish journalist, from Sweden, and he wrote I was like a sandbank except the sandbank was made of blubber. I gave an interview to a Canadian and he compared me to a beached whale. Ho ho. Tee hee. I mean I'm not entirely exonerating American journalists. One cub reporter from a newspaper over Dakota way described me as a cross between a giant squid and a hippopotamus lying by a river.

Of the foreign journalists, the ones who paid me most respect were the Third World country ones. They knew what it meant to be fat, because in their countries so many of them are like skeletons. A scrawny Indian journalist, from Bombay, in this baggy lightweight suit, even said I was like the Buddha. I told him my Buddha joke. Why's Buddha always sitting staring at his belly? Answer: because his navel got a screw in it that's holding his backside on. We got on like old buddies till he asked me about the Tibetan music, and I couldn't really help him there. But he wrote a very respectful article, and the result was I started getting correspondence from people in India.

I got bored, sometimes. Bored with the journalists, bored with the visitors, even more bored with the droning of the Tibetan monks. Thinking of what I was earning was some compensation, but in mid-late afternoon the hands of the clock sometimes seemed almost to stop moving round, time went so slow. Here's a story from just one such afternoon, when I'd drifted into a catnap, as I occasionally did, and woke to hear a little girl asking her momma, in a shrill voice, "Is it alive?" and the momma saying, "Sure, honey. Sure. Not so loud. Don't wake him."

The girl said, "But what is it?"

"Wha'd'ya mean, honey, what is it? What's what?"

The girl was eight years old, I guess. I listened pretty intently.

"Well, that's him," said the momma. "That's the mountain."

"What?"

"That's the man. The man-mountain. The fattest man in America."

I watched the girl's face as she studied me. It was a picture of disbelief, as the phrase goes. She was one of those chubby-cheeked little girls who looks like there's a pecan nut sitting in each cheek. "What is it really, Momma?"

"It's a man, honey. Truly. That's the man we've come and paid to see. Look, you can see him breathing," the woman pointed. "Look, there's his feet. You can see the toes."

The girl came close, staring. She was leaning across the rail, toward my feet. She gave a sudden gasp, "Ahhh," and recoiled, then looked more closely again. "Mom, the nails! Can you see? And the little toe? It's scary. It's so scary."

"It's amazing!" the woman said. "It's quite beautiful, in a way. It has a real presence."

"It's gross!" the girl said. Her gaze moved up my legs, and over my belly to my face. "It's just gruesome. It's horrible. I mean, can you imagine?"

"Honey, I think it's stupendous," said the mother. "I have never seen anything like it in my life. It is just— beyond—" she broke off. "Look, can you see? He's been reading *The Grapes of Wrath*. That's a good American book."

"I don't believe it," the girl repeated. She seemed to be inspecting me as if some deception was being practiced. "Why d'you think he's sleeping? He could be awake."

"No. He can't be." There was a pause, then the woman turned to the security guard. "Is he awake? How can you tell?"

"I can't say, ma'am," he answered her. "It's not for me to say."

"Can he stand up? Can he walk?"

"I can't comment, ma'am."

They leaned closer. Then the girl poked me with a finger.

"I'm sorry, ma'am," the security guard intervened. "I don't believe you have touching rights on your tickets."

"We have to pay for touching rights?"

She knew that. She was just pretending.

"Yes, ma'am."

They remained contemplating me. The Buddhist monks

were chanting in the background. "I don't think he is awake," the girl concluded. "Mom? I don't think he is."

They were getting near the end of their three minutes, and I thought I might yawn, just to give them a frisson of excitement. You know, pretending to wake up. Then I had a much better idea. I knew it was kind of unprofessional conduct, and I'd never done it before and never did it subsequently, but this once I couldn't resist the temptation. I broke wind. A loud, low, powerful fart, beginning with an explosive bark and proceeding to an extended whirr. It must've lasted a good second and a half, if not longer.

Their jaws dropped. They straightened in horror and the mother grabbed the daughter and hustled her out of the Shrine. The security guard shook with laughter. He was really doubled up, his hands on his knees. "Yes sir, you gave it to her real good! Yes sir, you gave it her real good!" I didn't say a word, but inside I was laughing like a jelly. Of course, a moment later we had to compose ourselves for the next visitors.

That was unprofessional of me, I know that. It happened because I was bored, that's all. I never broke wind again, not on purpose; I held back till after the last visitors had gone for the day. Because in the end such an act was not only disrespectful to people who'd paid good American dollars; it also undermined my dignity, and destroyed the aura of reverence and respectability Hiram and I were attempting to create.

There's respect and respect. It can go too far, maybe. Right at the start of the first tape I believe I mentioned this woman in red pumps who came back time and time again, caressing my flesh. She always came in early afternoon, very regular, and in a weird way I got to look forward to her visits, just wondering what she was going to do next. There was a kind of tension in the air when she came in the Shrine and knelt down at my side, at least after it stopped just being a matter of stroking. What happened was that one afternoon her mouth went down to give my skin her usual quick good-bye kiss, but instead of doing so she seemed to hesitate. She looked up at me quickly, with a flash of her eyes. That was the first moment she'd acknowledged my existence as a human being. Of course I was wearing dark glasses; she couldn't tell if I was watching. But maybe she could tell, from the angle of my head, or maybe she just guessed. Anyway, the tip of her tongue came out and seemed to moisten the flesh with little licks, and the next moment she'd taken a little bit of slack flesh in her teeth. I was thinking, hey, lady, are you going to bite me? What now? And, well, she holds this little fillet of flesh in her teeth and looks up at me. Knowing as she's bent over I can see her breasts down her blouse. And knowing I know she knows. She didn't bite me properly, but she slowly brought her teeth together till they were nearly touching. I checked after she'd gone and you could see the tooth marks and the gaps between the indentations of the tooth marks. Nor did the marks go. They were still there, only a little faded, when she returned the next afternoon. And she went straight back to them. Renewed them, if you like. Had a fresh nibble.

I didn't mind too much. It didn't bother me. The way she looked up at me like that gave a certain eroticism to the moment, though from her perspective I'm not sure whether it was what she intended. Maybe she was hoping to hurt me just enough to get a reaction, I don't know. As I say, I'm pretty good at not reacting. Whatever was going on in her mind was probably pretty complex, you'd need a team of psychoanalysts to tell you what it was, but it seemed to me she regarded me primarily as a devotional object. Because that wasn't the end of it. Another day she kneels and spreads out a hand, near the waistband of my pants. And suddenly I hear this little click. Or clip. I couldn't see what she's doing, but after she's gone I find a little piece of my pants've been cut out. That clip is the clip of scissors. Next time she comes in I'm watching pretty carefully. She kneels down as usual, biting her bottom lip, positioning her body so the security guard can't see what she's doing, and quickly slides a pair of scissors out the arm of her blouse. Then she tries to cut off a piece of one of my toenails. She was very quick about it. I didn't say anything but I motioned to the security guard, and he showed her out.

I had to prevent her coming to see me after that. She was refused admission. I was half sorry, I'd come to look forward to her visits, but it'd got too intrusive. Too dangerous. I felt maybe she was getting obsessed, and next thing she might've pulled out a knife. Who knows? Of course, when I told Hiram about the nail-cutting he laughed: "Call it a goddamn shrine, whaddya expect?" His mind ran to the commercial implications: like charging an

113

extra premium for biting, or selling little sprigs of my hair. Like bits of the True Cross, he said, the nails, the blood of Jesus, what's it called, the Holy Grail. "Why don't we sell vials of your blood?" He wasn't kidding, either; he was serious. I mean I didn't like the sound of it at all. I didn't even like the hair-selling idea too much. What if it took off? I'd be bald. No problem, says Hiram, we'll use someone else's hair. Who's to know?

Hiram was always like that, very business-focused. That was something he picked up at Cornell. On the subject of baldness, he used to talk about the old American bald eagle. An eagle, Hiram used to say, it doesn't have wide vision but it has concentration, it has focus. It can be half a mile up and it can see the twitch of a buck rabbit on the ground. Now he maintained, and I agree, that's a good image for the way the most successful people have achieved their success, by focusing intensively. That's one reason why I reckon the bald eagle is the best possible symbol for the United States of America, the other reason being that it's the most powerful bird in the skies. It's not afraid of anyone, certainly not of the Soviet Union.

Anyway it didn't work, the sprigs of hair. We tried it for a month and then abandoned it. That's what it's like in business, you try an idea, sometimes it works, sometimes it doesn't. The worst thing is not trying because you're afraid of failing. I believe that, I really do. If the American pioneers had been afraid of failing they'd have never got anywhere, they'd never even have set out on the *Mayflower*. They'd still be sitting in Plymouth, England, staring at the ocean.

114

The way I saw it in those days, I was a businessman, my life was my business. The rest of my life? What d'you want to know? What's relevant? Everything stopped in the evenings. Nothing happened. There I was, alone in the house except for Tiger and Lincoln, with the Shrine and the cafeteria and the emporium. In a kind of limbo. Everything empty. House, head, soul. All empty. Sucked out, licked clean. Empty.

Times were it felt like a weird peace, after the hurly-burly of the day. Other times . . . other times I guess I was kind of lonely. I was too fat to get a cab to go downtown, so I was marooned. There were the phones, but I had no one to phone, except for the pizza company. So that's what I did. Send out for pizzas. Pizzas and pizzas. And fetch myself chilled beer from the cafeteria. Those long and empty evenings, when others were laughing and talking and making love, I was just eating and drinking and channel-hopping.

One evening, however, I had a visitor. A big, blue, air-conditioned Cadillac slides to a halt outside the house, and guess who steps out? It was Uncle Bobby and a new wife. They'd been motoring to Houston from Fort Worth, where they now lived. Well I couldn't get over it because, for a start, she was so young. Mid twenties, that's all, whereas he was twice that. In addition, she turned out to be an Indian!

"Michael," says Uncle Bobby in that slow, gruff voice of his, "meet Anya."

He was in a big floppy kind of suit, very gray and floppy; I mean he looked like an elephant. Whereas she was beautiful, really beautiful. How Uncle Bobby ever persuaded her to hitch up with him beats me. Well, I invited them in. I thought about offering Uncle Bobby a beer, but knowing his susceptibility to liquor I guessed better not, so we drank coke.

What I discovered was, she was quite an educated person, for an Indian. By that I don't mean all Indians are ill-educated. I don't want to sound prejudiced. I mean there is a lot of prejudice out there, believe me, and you can understand it historically. A hundred and fifty years ago, before the railroad came, when Constant was not much bigger than a village, the folk there were marauded by Indians, they went in fear of their lives, a ranger regiment had to be brought in to protect them.

All I'm saying is, they called by. Uncle Bobby was in grand form, he was like the cat who'd got the cream, and he kept putting his arm round Anya's shoulders and kissing her on her ears and neck, and chewing her earlobes. I mean he practically chewed one of them off, it seemed to me. She kept trying to push him off while saying "Stop it, Bobby! Stop it, please," but in that playful laughing kind of way so you knew he wouldn't stop it and I felt kind of sorry for her, specially when he began mauling her breasts. "Don't embarrass me, Bobby," she kept saying, "you're embarrassing me," but it made no difference to Uncle Bobby. He kept winking at me and mauling her body. As I say, he was the cat who'd got the cream all right except, as I say, he looked like an elephant. I could imagine him in the zoo in Houston, with big ears and these curving tusks and a long floppy trunk curling between the bars, tweaking the feather boa on this big fat lady's hat. When I was at school the kids used to call me Jumbo. Jum-bo! And Hiram called me Tusker—among other names. Well, all I'll say is, I may look kind of like an elephant, but you should see Uncle Bobby. You really should. Uncle Bobby's the original human elephant.

What I learnt, also, he'd got a new job as a gun salesman. That's why they were motoring to Houston, to attend a gun convention. The Cadillac was loaded with hunting rifles, pistols, shotguns; it was a motorized armory. "What's your weapon of choice, Michael?" he asked me in his deep, gruff voice. When I answered that most of the time I aimed on relying on passivity and good humor he told me I was crazy. "What you gonna do when some guy shows up one night threatening to blow holes in your ass?"

"There's nothing much to rob here," I said, "though not long ago a woman did try and cut off my toenails."

Anya laughed, but Uncle Bobby looks grave. "I'm not talking about robbin', I'm talking about shootin'," he says. "I'm talking about goddamn common sense. I'm talking about self-protection. If you ain't got no weapon, you ain't got no security. See here, this is what I carry," and reaching into his jacket pocket he brings out two little handguns. They looked like toys. "Light, easy, simple to use, won't wear a hole in your pants or your wallet."

He'd only been selling guns for about three months, but he had the sales pitch off by heart. He spun one of the guns on a finger. "Where's your peace of mind? You're

117

a well-known guy, you're famous. Anyone could decide to take a popshot at you. You need protection."

"Uncle Bobby, this isn't Houston," I say, "this is Drake. I have security staff here during the day."

"It's nights I'm talking about," he said. "You ought to be afraid at nights even if you're not. This is a nice property you've got here." He quoted some statistics at me about the rise in lawbreaking. Then he tried another tack. "Look," he said, "it's not only your right as a U.S. citizen to bear arms. It's your goddamn duty under the Second Amendment to the Constitution! If you don't exercise your right, it's not goddamn patriotic. If rights aren't exercised, they fall into goddamn disuse. Think of that, Michael."

I was interested by that line of argument. "Maybe," I said.

"No maybes. Straightforward fact. It's your duty as a patriot. What've you gotta lose? Okay, it's two hundred twenty dollars, but for you I'll make it a hundred fifty. Now, what's a hundred fifty against the possibility of being blown away by some pumped-up twelve-year-old kid wanting a bit of target practice?"

In the end I let myself be won over. Because Uncle Bobby's family, and family's family, and he'd taken the trouble to come to see me. The gun I bought was a Beretta revolver, if you want to know. It looked like a proper gun of the Wild West, that was why I liked it. Uncle Bobby was delighted. "That's a beautiful goddamn weapon you've chosen," he announced. "A be-yoo-ti-ful weapon. A piece of goddamn craftsmanship. But what you've really bought is peace of mind. Yes sir! You've bought yourself peace of mind. Ain't that so, baby?" he asks, pulling Anya over for another chew of her earlobes. In fact, he began eating his way down her neck, like you might eat down a kebab.

"I guess so," she says, in a soft singsong voice. "Bobby please!—" smoothing down her dress.

"Oh, Michael doesn't mind," he replies, sliding his hand between her legs and giving me another of his lurid winks.

Before they left, while she went to the bathroom, he said to me; "What d'ya reckon, eh? Pretty good ass on her, wouldn't ya say?"

"Very good," I said.

"Ya should see her without clothes on. Puts this Indian snake oil on her skin. Makes her wild." Uncle Bobby shuddered and rolled his eyes.

So away they went in their Cadillac and I was left with my Beretta. Which I've never fired as yet, though I guess I might have to one day, thinking of the shooting of Walter Giddins. I keep it in the bedroom, under a cushion. Does it make me feel more secure at nights? I don't reckon so. I reckon Providence is what gives you real protection, that's the best firearm anyone's ever going to have.

I haven't got much more to say just now, I don't reckon, but I hope all this is of some interest to your project. I'm glad if it's some assistance to you.

This is Michael, once Mickey, once the Fattest Man in the U. S. of A., signing off.

4

One of the difficulties with this tape is I can't recall exactly what I have and haven't said. However, I have listened back to the past half hour or so and I'd like to make one correction, with regard to telling you how I told the journalists I was a great fan of Mr. John Steinbeck's writing. That wasn't strictly true. I do have a copy of *Mice and Men*, given me by Hilary, my elder sister, who lives up in California, but I've never read it. I've never read any of John Steinbeck's books. Don't get me wrong, I'm told he's a fine American writer, and if I did read him I guess I'd like him; it's just I never got round to it. The whole thing about John Steinbeck started with that very first interview I gave, to the writer from the art magazine; she happened to see the copy of *Mice and Men* and asked me if I liked it. She seemed to want me to like it, so I said it was very interesting and the next thing I know her article's describing me as an avid reader who loves the works of John Steinbeck. An avid reader! Truth is I'm not an avid reader of anything. I used to read works about the early history of the United States, the Civil War and all that;

the pioneers, the railroaders, and I became pretty knowledgeable in that way, but that's all. I don't read much now, except the *Drake Chronicle* and the *Constant Bulletin*. Occasionally the *Reader's Digest*. But unfortunately, once word spread that I liked John Steinbeck, every journalist put it in their article, and fans started sending me letters asking for my opinion on this or that piece of John Steinbeck writing, and I even got a letter from a student doing a learned doctorate on John Steinbeck and the Meaning of America and stuff like that. It's an example of how if you don't keep tight control of things, they can unintentionally soon get out of hand. I didn't intend to mislead, just once it became established I couldn't back off. Usually I was able to fend off the questions easily enough, but occasionally I'd get a journalist who wanted to talk about nothing but John Steinbeck and who'd ask me things like who was my favorite John Steinbeck character and what did I think of the ending of *Grapes of Wrath*. Or, more often than not, the ending of some John Steinbeck novel I'd never even heard of. I'd bluff, but I don't know if I fooled everyone. It kind of embarrasses me now, thinking back.

There are plenty of other things I feel embarrassed about, that I probably ought to describe. Everyone makes mistakes in life, the most important thing is learning from them. But this is one of the more difficult parts of my account for me to tell. I need to stop for a moment to work out how to go on.

Okay. It was the winter of eighty-one, in the early

evening. A pleasant ordinary evening. The staff had gone home. I was relaxing in my bedroom, stroking Tiger while listening to the *Constant* "Country Hour" at high volume, when Hiram called in to see me. He didn't knock, least I didn't hear him, he just suddenly appeared. Smart as ever, he was always smart. Always the suit, the tie, the rings, the gold watch.

"Turn that shit off, would you Mickey?" was the first thing he said.

I didn't turn it off, but I did turn down the volume. "It's good country music," I said.

"Good country shit," he replied. He seated himself in a chair and crossed his legs. "What's that godawful curtain? Have you been wearing that all day?"

It was the robe my ma'd made for me. He'd never liked it. "No," I said, "I've just put it on. It's a cold night. I've a right to wear a robe if I want to wear a robe. It's not against the Constitution."

"Sure you have, sure you have," he said. "Everyone has a right to look a prick if they want to. You look like a fucking Moslem." He reached into a pocket and pulled out a toothpick and started picking his teeth. "Mickey, I've been with old Denison."

Mr. Denison was the accountant we used. He came from Tyler. He had baggy eyes and a long sad face.

"How're we doing?" I asked.

"So-so," he said. "We need to hike up the publicity."

Then he brought up this notion we ought to relocate. Drake was too far off of the beaten path, it was a hick town. We ought to move to Florida, set up in Orlando, cream off the Disney World trade. The second Mickey, ya might say. Then we'd be making real money. At the moment it was Mickey Mouse money, Hiram said.

"Maybe," I said. "I guess you're right."

"I know I'm right. On business grounds there's no fucking argument," he said.

I wasn't convinced. Okay, we only had thirty-five thousand visitors the year before, and the business wasn't big like Disney World was big, it wouldn't never be. Not in that league. But, the thing was, I liked Drake. I liked it being small, I liked the folk here, I liked the atmosphere. And I liked the house. I liked how the timbers creaked and groaned with the wind, or in the morning when the sun hit and heated them up after a cold night. I liked the view over the town to the hills beyond.

So I told him I'd think about it.

"Have a think, have a think," he said. "If you want to really break in big-time—"

"Okay."

He was leaning forward, the front part of his arms on his knees, seeming to reflect.

"D'ya ever get lonely, Colonel?"

That's one thing he'd started to call me, Colonel. I don't know why.

"D'ya ever get lonely, Colonel?"

"What?" I said. "What, with thirty thousand folk a year coming through my house?"

"After they've gone. D'ya ever feel in need of company?

D'ya ever think, why not spend a few dollars, get some chicken?"

I wasn't sure what he meant. He seemed to eye me. Then he laughed and dug the toe of his shoe into my side.

"Ya fat slob. You're not as fucking dumb as you make out."

"I hope I don't look dumb," I said.

"Oh, my Christ." He laughed again. "Why not? I'm gonna make a call."

He went and made it.

"Who did you call?"

"No one." He picked up his hat. "See ya, Mickey. By the by, a friend of mine might pop round to see you later, if you're thinking of going out."

"I don't ever go out," I said. "What's he called? What friend?"

"Sure you don't, sure you don't," he said. "Stupid me, I was forgetting. Well, see ya, Colonel."

"What's he called?" I shouted after him.

"She," he shouted back. "She wants to meet you. She's a big fan."

A couple of hours later there's this knock on the door. Not on my private door, but on the main entrance door. I wouldn't normally answer it but I'm expecting a load of pizza from downtown so I hauled myself along. And this girl's there, in a leather coat. She was quite thin, and had short-cropped hair, and she looked kind of lost and cold. It was quite a cold night, there were stars. There was a cab behind her in the dark. I mean it wasn't actually dark because we kept the Fattest Man sign going through the night, so the darkness kept changing color every few seconds. So this girl was standing there, in a leather coat, and it was going green, red, yellow, gold, purple, the lights shining on the leather of the coat . . . when I say she was a girl I mean she might have been twenty or eighteen or something. Or younger, more like sixteen. I don't know.

"Hi," she said, then she seemed to give a kind of gulp. (She'd suddenly realized how big I was, I guess.) She took a step back. "Christ. Christ."

"What is it? It's closed."

"Mr. Cutler sent me. He said to give you his compliments."

She was standing there, and it seemed only polite, since she was a fan, so I let her in. It's not relevant, but her name was Elizabeth, if you want to know.

"How d'you know Mr. Cutler?" I asked.

"Well, I do," she said, "I know him. He sent me up. D'you mind if I smoke?"

"I'd sooner you didn't," I said.

That was one thing I should've mentioned, I never allowed people who came to see me to smoke. The only person who always smoked was Hiram, I couldn't stop him, but I never allowed any of the staff or the visitors to smoke. Back in the fifties I believe there was a guy called Fat Albert Jackson with a sprawling belly like me, and people used to come and look at it, and they didn't always believe it was real. To check, they used to tap hot ash on his flesh. Not a pleasant thought. But there're other

reasons why I put a ban on tobacco. For one, the fire risk—
the house being wooden. For another, I don't personally
happen to enjoy the smell of tobacco. And there's the health
aspect. In Martha's family cigarettes are known as coffin
nails, c-o-f-f-i-n nails, on account of the fact they make you
cough as well as killing you. She's full of things like that.

So I said, "I'd sooner you didn't." Then I asked Elizabeth
how come she was a friend of Hiram's.

"Hiram?" she said.

"Hiram, Mr. Cutler."

"Oh. Sure. Hiram, is that his name?" She obviously
didn't know Hiram that well, seeing as she didn't know
his first name. But she was looking around her. She had
come through the main entrance, as I say, so now she was
looking at herself in the distorting mirrors. "This is so
crazy," she said.

"You haven't been here before?"

"I've only been in Drake a couple of weeks."

I took her through to the Shrine. Tiger came up to greet
her, real friendly, but she didn't take too much notice. She
wasn't a cat-lover. "Where do I put my coat?" she asked.

I took her coat and hung it up in the closet in my
bedroom. She wasn't wearing very much under the coat,
by the way. She was wearing a short skirt and a kind of
orange T-shirt. I wasn't surprised she was cold. Folk sometimes think it's always warm down here, but in the winter
you'd be surprised how cold it gets.

"So why'd you come to Drake?" I asked.

She shrugged. "Reasons." She didn't want to tell me. I

126

thought maybe she'd come on account of me. "Where do we go?" she asked.

I didn't know what she meant. I mean it was embarrassing, the whole thing. I'm embarrassed telling you about it now. I know it sounds naïve but I still didn't realize what was going on, I still thought it must be because she was a fan.

"This is the Shrine," I said.

"Sure," she said.

It was really naïve of me. I didn't know why she was here, I thought she was just a fan. I said, "Have you got a camera?"

She frowned. "I don't know about cameras."

"I mean," I said, "I can give you a signed photo if you like. Or there're posters. D'you want to see the emporium?"

"Well," she said, "I told the cab driver I'd be half an hour, see."

"Okay," I said.

"So maybe we ought—y'know—" she kept looking round her.

Well, then the doorbell rang again and it was the pizza order.

I was in a quandary about that. One thing I never like, have I mentioned this? I never like fans seeing me eating, it's a kind of sensitive point. I don't like *anyone* to see me eating, come to think of it, aside from Martha. But pizza has to be eaten hot, a cold pizza is . . . I went for the pizzas, and there was the cab, sure enough, waiting, and I carried the pizzas back into the Shrine. She wasn't there. She'd gone through to my private bedroom, and to my amazement she'd taken off her skirt and T-shirt. I was amazed. I put down the pizzas and then she came over and parted my robe. I was amazed, I truly was. Tell the truth, I was flattered. I'd never been with a woman before, if you discount that incident with the hawk-eyed old chambermaid at the Ranelagh Grand.

I don't want to encourage prurience, so I won't go into detail. It's too embarrassing even to think of. Let's say there are certain problems if you're quite as fat as I am, but you can get round them, and she was quite . . . she was quite inventive. I was pretty relieved I wasn't impotent, tell the truth. It's one of the possible complications of diabetes. But she didn't seem to enjoy it too much, and afterwards she didn't hang around for nothing. I ask if she'd like to stay for some pizza, but she just slips on her T-shirt, whips her coat off the rail, and shoots out the door in a snap of fingers, like she's got some business appointment waiting.

I never saw her again, not even once, but other girls came up to the house, mostly on Saturdays. Sometimes other days of the week, it depended what I was feeling like. But once I'd got the taste for it I couldn't get enough of it. I forgot everything I'd ever known about clean living, everything my ma and pa'd ever taught me and all those lessons at the Baptists, and I just gave in to my carnal desires. There was one called Naomi, who was black, I couldn't get enough of her, I sent for her seven nights in a row. She was very, what's the word, she was very accommodating. She always wore white, I used to dream about her. The white against the black. Like she was the ultimate *nègre en chemise*, the nigger in a nightshirt incarnate. There was something about the blackness of her skin. Her fingernails were pink. The inside of her mouth was pink. But there was a kind of glossiness to her skin like eggplant and I used to dream about her all day; when people came in I'd be lounging on my beanbags and pretending to read John Steinbeck and all I'd be thinking of was Naomi. Then I got bored with her. I guess I decided maybe she didn't like me as a person. At the start I reckoned she did like me, but maybe she was pretending, like I pretended to read John Steinbeck. Because afterwards, she'd never stay to talk, not even for a few minutes. Same with the other girls. They'd always go off like they were in a hurry to get someplace. It was a shame. When my ma was here running the place I could talk to her, now I didn't have no one. I could've done with some half-good conversation sometimes in the evening, instead of watching the television and eating pizza. You can't talk to a television.

The regular girl I got after that, and the only girl who ever stayed to talk, was Maria. She was Puerto Rican, a Puerto Rican girl. Poor as hell. Her skin was the color of a milky chocolate, and she had long black hair, and I liked the feel of it trailing across my belly. Her mouth was perfect. But she was very, very thin, that was the weird thing, so thin I could see all her ribs. Sometimes we'd stay in the Shrine, instead of going to the bedroom, and as we

129

made love on the beanbags I'd watch her in the mirror and I'd see all these ribs and my big fat hands moving over her and I'd feel sorry she was so thin. If I could've given up some of my surplus flesh I'd've done it. I liked her and I guessed she liked me. Two or three times she stayed for beer and pizza afterwards. She liked very hot, spicy pizzas, with chili. I didn't eat that much, but I liked watching her eating, thinking of the goodness she was getting from the food. It was almost better than making love to her, it felt kind of deeper.

One night Maria came in with her face bruised real bad. Swollen up. She wouldn't tell me what had happened, who'd done it, but then she began weeping.

I said, "Maria! Who did it?"

"What does it matter?"

"It matters to me."

She said nothing. She just took off her clothes like normal, still weeping.

"Have a smoke," I said. I knew she liked smoking, so I was making an exception.

She sat hunched, not wearing anything, with her skinny shoulders. The bones just sticking out. Her hand trembling as she smoked the cigarette. She was young; I felt real sorry for her. She couldn't hardly hold the cigarette.

I asked, "Is it money?"

"No."

"What then?"

"Ain't anything."

"Must be something."

"Ain't anything."

"I'll get you some money if that'd help."

She didn't say anything.

"We might be able to fix up some employment here. Like waitering in the cafeteria. We need another waitress. If you like, I'll speak to Hiram. Y'know Hiram? Mr. Cutler?"

"No," she said. "No. Christ, no. Waitering? Of course I know him. He's a louse."

That wasn't actually what she said, I won't repeat what she actually said.

"Hiram's okay," I said. "Isn't he? Hiram's okay."

I didn't know what it was about. There was something she wasn't telling me, she wouldn't say. For a moment the thought did cross my mind maybe it was Hiram'd hit her, but I didn't think that was possible. Why would he have hit her? She was so thin. I mean, I got quite fond of Maria. I really did. Tiger liked her too. Used to run up to her when she came in the door, rub his flanks against her legs.

I guess I was pretty naïve, all in all. I was blinded by fame. Fame . . . fame was what I'd always wanted, more than being rich, and I was getting there. In a year or two I reckoned folk'd be dreaming about me, all over America, like they dreamed about the President. I'd be inhabiting people's dreams! Like sleeping with the whole nation, every night. And there'd be TV documentaries, talkshows, billboards. I was getting there now. I knew it, in my heart. I knew it when I watched the admiration of people who visited me, or when I looked outside on an evening and saw the illuminated sign crying my existence. Purple, green, red, yellow, gold. Purple, green, red, yellow, gold. Sometimes I felt I was there already: a living legend, an American success story. A giant. The man-mountain, the balloon, the king; the pioneer.

I guess I was fooling myself. Maybe. Maybe I was never so very famous. But I did begin to have imitators, more than a half a dozen, in other parts of the States. I didn't realize until I was shown this article in *Round America* magazine. Just three or four paragraphs, mentioning me and this guy in Birmingham, Alabama, who weighed seven hundred and ninety-five pound and who—inspired by my example—had also started opening his doors to the public. The article was called "The Commercialization of Flesh." It wasn't much of an article, and whatever there was in relation to me was mostly inaccurate, based on old out-of-date copy. That's what I'd half come to expect.

It was Hiram who showed me the article. He came into my bedroom, drinking whiskey and smoking a cigarette. He seemed to believe that I ought to be concerned.

"Hey, Colonel! What if this guy in Birmingham gets as heavy as you? What's his name?"

"C'mon," I said. "He's a featherweight. Could you put out your cigarette?"

He ignored me. "Mickey, it's very important we safeguard your position. If you're not number one, you're nothing, you're nowhere. We're in a competitive situation. We can't tolerate competitors. We can't afford to be complacent."

I said that I took a different, more relaxed view: I saw

them as colleagues engaged in the same line of work. Besides, imitation was the sincerest form of flattery. Anyone who's successful gets imitated, sure as eggs is eggs. I asked him to put out his cigarette again.

"You don't know what you're talking sometimes, Mickey," Hiram answered. "You're talking bullshit. You need to get eating."

"I eat enough as it is. I am what I am."

"You need to eat more. You need to aim higher."

"What you mean, aim higher?"

"A thousand pound. Set that as your target, fat man. Then we'll be sitting pretty. Make yourself the first man to hit a thousand pound. I mean, you're only a hundred or so short."

He was in a sullen mood, I saw. He took a sip of his whiskey.

"If this sonafabitch, what's his name . . . "

"He won't catch up . . . "

"—If he does you know what, don't you? You're finished. No one's gonna pay to see the second fattest man in America. You won't get a thousand people through the doors in a year."

I resented that. I wasn't in so good a temper either. "Look," I said, "if I get to a thousand I get to a thousand. May I point out that I've never claimed to be the heaviest man in America? I've only ever claimed to be the fattest."

"That's bull," he said. "Fattest, heaviest, what's the difference?" He stared into his whiskey. "What's his name? Gimme the article!"

133

I held on to the article. "His name's Douglas."

"Douglas. Douglas. I bet he's eating like crazy. I bet he's eating fit to bust all day every day. He'll beat you, Mickey. If you rest on your laurels, he'll beat you."

I recall that phrase, resting on your laurels. What's it mean, resting on your laurels? What are laurels? I was resting on my side.

He took a drag on his cigarette. It fussed me. We weren't in the living room, we were in the bedroom. My bedroom! Jesus!

After a while he said, more calmly, "Well, I suppose we could just make you heavier. Jack you up a few pound. That'd do."

"What're you going to do? You can't just make me heavier."

"We'll *say* you're heavier. We won't *do* anything. Just say it. Tell the world. Mickey is now a thousand pound!"

"I don't want to tell an untruth."

"No one'll ever find out," he said. "If we say you're a thousand pound, who's ever going to know otherwise?"

"I'm not telling an untruth."

"Don't you worry—I'll tell it for you. Then you keep on feeling nice and white and pure, fat man."

He said it in a very pleasant voice, but I didn't much like the tone. I was a little hurt at him calling me fat man, particularly as he was drinking my liquor.

"Hiram," I said, "if the business needs developing, why don't we go on tour?"

"On tour? What tour?"

134

"Anywhere. Round the United States. You're always saying we ought to relocate to Florida."

He looked at me quite sharply. "A tour? For how long? Jesus." He started to laugh. "Think of the costs transporting you round the country? Jesus." Then he fell silent, thinking. "Where'd you exhibit yourself?"

"Plenty of art galleries," I said. "I'm serious."

There was a long silence. He laughed. He took another drag on his cigarette. "You're really serious?"

"Sure. If that's what the business needs, that's what it needs."

Another long silence. "Okay," he said. "Okay. We could do it. But you'd need to put on more weight. Get to nine hundred and fifty pound, at the minimum. And it'd need proper planning and marketing."

"I want to be marketed as art," I said. "My body is my art, you know?"

He laughed again. I felt riled.

"Hiram, that's what you're always saying!"

"And so I am, so I am, Colonel. So I am. You're great art. You're a modern masterpiece. Ya fat slob."

I ignored his tone. "Also," I said, "I want to start some-place like Charleston, or Savannah."

"Why? Savannah?"

"The photo tour of me started in Savannah."

"Yeah?"

"Or Charleston," I said.

Hiram stood up and went to the window and chucked his cigarette out. "We'll need a fucking big truck," he said.

135

"With a big ramp. I wonder what the zoos move elephants about in." He kind of mimed an elephant's trunk at me and made a trumpeting noise. "Okay, tusker. I'll see what I can cook up."

I resented his lack of respect, but I figured we were tied together in the business, and in business terms I calculated a tour was a logical and sensible proposition. Sure it was a gamble. I'd be away from Drake for a number of months and some folk wouldn't know and they'd show up and go away disappointed. I'd keep open the cafeteria and the emporium, but I'd have to keep on paying the wages of my staff. But the way I saw it, risk-taking is part of the American mentality. Look at the Pilgrim Fathers, risking their lives. They set off blind in the *Mayflower* to cross the great uncharted expanse of the Atlantic Ocean with only their prayers and faith in Providence to guide them on their way and support them in adversity, and they ended up founding a new civilization, the greatest in the history of mankind.

All you need at the start is one smart idea. Like Thomas Edison, inventor of the lightbulb. But then, tenacity. Tenacity and drive and application. And you need your quota of luck, I don't minimize that. People sometimes say you have to manufacture your own luck, and I'd agree with that, but also you hope to count on a little luck falling into your lap. That's my opinion, take it as you will.

What you do in business, you don't ignore the risks, but you feed them along with the rewards into the overall program. Also you examine previous models. In my case, there'd been the success of the photographic Fat Man tour run by Eddie Dukes, with whom, incidentally, I've remained in touch, although now he's working up in New York.

But in this proposal for a tour I confess I had more than mere business considerations in mind. Back in February eighty-two a letter had arrived on pink notepaper.

Dear Mickey,

I have read several articles about you in such magazines as Hearth and Home *and the* American Kitchen *and I was especially struck by your remark that fat people are only fat in relation to thin people. I think this is very true. For years, as a fat American woman, I have experienced much prejudice at the hands of those who fail to comprehend the needs of fat people. On account of this prejudice I suffer from low self-esteem, which has adversely and significantly affected my quality of life. I have had serious problems in finding paid employment ever since I got stuck in a revolving door, and my last boyfriend left me, saying that I was too obese. Now my dietary consultant wishes to reduce my weight by putting me on a special crash diet, called the Survival Diet. I don't know if you have heard of this diet, but it is a very severe one which involves long periods of fasting. But if it is not wrong to be fat, why should I bother?*

I should be most grateful for your advice. I am 23 years of age and I weigh 315 pounds, and I live with my mother and father in the small town of Dorchester, outside of

137

Charleston. I have never visited you in Drake, although I long to do so; it is one of my most cherished ambitions.

I know how many letters you must receive, and how pressed you must be for time. I do sincerely hope that you will not mind my writing to you in these terms.

Yours respectfully,

Martha Watts

I get lots of letters but this one interested me, I don't know why. Instinct, or something. Maybe it was the revolving door. Maybe the mention of Charleston, with its railroad connections. So I didn't just get one of the administrative staff to send off the standard reply; instead I wrote back myself, longhand:

Dear Martha,

Thank you very much for your letter, which I enjoyed reading.

I'm sorry about your problem with the revolving door and I sympathize deeply with your situation as a fat woman. I too have experienced stigmatization, from sections of the media and from the state authorities down here. I too have had employment difficulties. And I too once believed my body size was a problem. Now, I may say, I see it differently, as an opportunity!

I cannot truly comment on your individual circumstances, but three hundred pounds is not so very heavy, and I would beware of the Survival Diet. Although it is not one that I know, it sounds not unlike a diet I once heard of called the Starvation Diet. The whole of society is doing its best to make us conform in the ways we think as well as in the ways we look. Society would like to turn us into clones with a standard body weight, whereas I believe the richness of this world we live in lies in its diversity. I also firmly believe that there is nothing wrong with being fat, and that if everyone was fat it would be thought odd to be thin. If it is your destiny to be fat as you are, then to diet would be to go against your destiny.

I enclose a photograph of myself, and also a voucher for a free visit, with my very best wishes.

Yours truly,

Mickey
(The Fattest Man in America)

She wrote back:

Dear Mickey,

I am so grateful for your letter. Truly it has been a weight off my mind, and I feel comforted and inspired and happier with my body than I have been for years. I have decided not to diet, but to eat according to my desires.

The time I got stuck in the revolving door was in a department store in Charleston when I was hoping to buy clothes, which I'm sure you too have found is not easy for a fat person. I know it sounds comic, but I found it an *embarrassing and humiliating experience. Since receiving your letter I feel I am no longer alone in my situation, and this is a great comfort to me.*

I shall treasure your photograph. Just looking at it I can tell what a very warm personality you have. I was truly excited to see it, and I would love to meet you some-time in order to express my gratitude in person, and I am grateful for the voucher.

I enclose a photograph of me.

With very best wishes,
Yours most truly,

Martha

The photograph showed a young and very luscious woman, with a pleasant face. She was certainly fat, no doubt about that, though as she was wearing a kind of robe like the one my ma'd made for me, but Oriental, with snakes and dragons and fishes and things, like this one I'm wearing now, it wasn't so easy to see her dimensions.

I wrote back:

Dear Martha,
I received your photograph with great pleasure, you look a lovely person and I too hope circumstances may permit us to meet. I envy you that you have the good fortune to live so near Charleston, the city from which the first proper railroad was built in the United States. I wonder if you

have ever visited Branchville, where I believe there is an
excellent railroad museum by the name of the Branchville
Railroad Shrine . . .

She wrote back:

Dear Mickey,
Sure I know Branchville! I have an aunt who used to
live near there, my Aunt May (my mother's sister), and
we used to drive past the station building . . .

We corresponded a great deal after that, we must have
exchanged a dozen or more letters. We discovered we had
a good amount of common ground, for example we had the
same taste in music. She was a big country fan like me
and had a record collection with valuable old recordings
by legends like Gene Autry and Roy Acuff, including the
original recording of Roy Acuff singing "The Great
Speckle Bird", recorded in nineteen thirty-six. I sent her
a framed copy of the Big Mickey poster, and the Mickey
dishcloth and one of the china Mickey models, and in turn
she sent me more photographs of herself, including one
of her in a Wild West costume with pistols and a Stetson,
and boots. Leather boots, knee-high. And a tasselled jacket.
I used to pore over those images minutely looking at all
the tiny detail and wondering who'd taken them for her,
the photos. I felt pretty jealous . . . Some of them were
taken outside, in a kind of backyard area by a barbecue,
and others beside a kind of red station wagon. One photo-

graph was taken indoors, in her kitchen. It looked like a nice, bright kitchen, very clean and well-equipped, with gleaming saucepans and a food processor. There was a knife rack on the wall, and by the knife rack was my poster, the life-size poster, and by the poster she was standing, smiling, knife in hand.

★

The business of setting up the tour took a long time. We formulated a provisional schedule, which we then had to reformulate and reformulate. It became a two-stage tour, the first stage being the East Coast and the second the West, divided by six months back in Drake. On the East Coast route, I was to start in Orlando, then travel up to Charleston and then Washington, D.C., and New York. About six weeks in each city. We discussed Pittsburgh, but Hiram didn't reckon Pittsburgh was right, I don't know why. We booked the art galleries. I say we, in reality I did nothing, I left it up to Hiram, but I kept pretty much in touch with what was going on. The gallery owners were mostly pretty receptive and keen to have me, Hiram said. He showed me a photograph of the studio in Orlando where I'd be going, with whitewashed walls and floodlights. Also the promo leaflet. It had a shot of me in my Stars and Stripes pants. It said: MICKEY, THE 1,000-POUND ALL-AMERICAN MARVEL. A thousand pound! I was annoyed about that but it was already printed.

The tour was to begin in February eighty-three and run

through to the last Saturday of May that year. Travel was fixed up, too. I'd be traveling in a quite luxurious coach, the door having been modified so that I could be fit through, and staying in five-star hotels. I insisted on that. I didn't want three-star hotels or four-star. I wanted to stay in the kinds of hotel the rich and famous stayed in. I wanted to have some crummy bellhop carrying my bags up in the elevator.

I was pretty excited, it was a long time since I'd been away from home, or even down into Drake, and I was looking forward to it. The cats were a concern. Hiram felt I should have the cats with me, he said they represented an integral part of the act—it was kind of touching, he said, putting someone as fat as me alongside a thin slinky creature like a cat, and made for great photos—but I wasn't so sure. Cats don't like traveling. I gave in, however. Partly as I didn't have anyone to take care of them in my absence, partly because I wanted to introduce the cats to Martha. Round this time we were writing letters to each other every two or three days, and she said she'd be definitely coming to view me when the show reached Charleston.

I'd think of how she was in her house, and I was in my house. We were divided by desert, forest, brush, mountain, city, lake, but I'd think how my feelings were pouring toward her across America like a beam of shooting light. She was at the other end of the beam, huge and smiling, radiant, and it didn't seem like any distance at all.

143

5

It's a few days since I've been doing any recording on account of the fact I've busy with preparations for a certain event, which I intend shortly to describe, in addition to which I've been having more tests for my diabetes. Monitoring glucose levels, checking the blood pressure, that kind of thing. They examine my feet and legs for sores and calluses. I'm not worried, if there's anything much wrong I guess Dr. Coughlan'll let me know. He's a good doctor. Getting to the clinic takes some doing since I can't get in an ordinary cab, but Zoe, my baby sister, she comes along from Constant in her truck and drives me there. I quite enjoy it when I'm there, tell the truth, the nurses are good, I'd recommend it to anyone. We come back via the G. T. Robbins grocery store, lay in some provisions.

On the previous tape I was talking about the "Fat America" tour. It was Hiram's idea to call it that, the "Fat America" tour. I kind of liked it, the thought of America itself being fat, a fat country. Fat and happy and prosperous, I'd say. Contented with itself. Well, I was about to experience a distinct decline in self-content. It was in

144

the summer of eighty-two, during my midday meal, when I heard this commotion outside the Shrine. Voices raised, that kind of thing. Nothing too serious. Presently one of the security guys knocked on the door. "Lady here to see you, sir," he called out, and for a moment I thought it might've been the woman in the red pumps. I'd been kind of troubled about her. Then he continued, "Your sister, sir," and a moment later Hilary, my older sister, who lives up north in Richmond, California, walks in. I was real pleased to see her, family's family, flesh and blood.

"Michael, I haven't got a ticket," she says.

"You don't need a ticket," I say, putting my food aside. "Hi!"

She's very smart. She's wearing a kind of pale green pantsuit and a string of pearls and pearl earrings. She kisses me on the forehead and sits with her handbag on her knees and her knees together.

"How's life?" I say.

"Fine," Hilary says. "Sure, everyone's fine."

"Ma?"

"She's just fine."

"How's Jack?"

"He's fine."

"Has he located any dinosaur bones lately?"

"Well," she said, "he's in Arizona right now, as it happens, on an expedition."

It's funny, he's always in Arizona. Or he's at a conference someplace. New York, Chicago, London, he spends his time flying off to conferences. I said, "What does he do with them when he finds them? I mean, does he just stick 'em in his pack or something?"

"Something like that," she said, with a smile.

I laughed. "It's a weird way of earning a living."

"You think that's weird?" she asked. "What about you? You're the weird one, look at you. But, no, he's fine, thank you. He sends his best wishes. The kids're fine too. They're with Zoe in Constant right now. Zoe sends her love."

"And Ma's fine?" I asked. I'd already asked that, I know, but I wanted to find out more.

"Oh, you know Ma," she says. "Same as ever. How long've we got before people start coming through?"

I told her: about fifteen minutes. Then I couldn't think what to say. Trouble with Hilary, because she's five years older than me, and because she moved up to Richmond, we've never been as close as we might've been. I'm much closer to Zoe. Hilary always seemed almost grown up to me when young. Anyway, I couldn't think what to say and at that moment I couldn't even recall the names of Frank and Anita, her two kids, so I asked her about her glee club. I should've mentioned that she sings with the University Glee Club. She does, I'm not kidding. She's a soprano. They travel all over the States, singing glees. I mean I think that's maybe how she met Jack, her husband, the fossil hunter. They're both very keen on glee singing.

"Oh, that's fine," she says. "We're going on a tour to Pennsylvania in the fall."

"What are you singing?"

"Michael," she says, "you're not interested."

146

"I am," I say, doing my best to look interested. "Sure I'm interested."

"Well, we'll be singing a wide range of songs. Popular, sacred, traditional, patriotic. Right across the range." She named some song by, I think it was Felix someone or other. "I know it's not all your sort of music. One thing we're singing you would know is 'Chattanooga Choo Choo.' Michael, I wish you'd take off those glasses," she said, "I can't see your eyes."

I did so. "What're the patriotic songs?"

"Oh, just the usual ones," she says.

"'America, the Beautiful'?"

"Sure," she says. "And 'The Star-Spangled Banner.' But I know this is more to your taste." And digging into her handbag she gives me a present, gift-wrapped, with a silver sash.

I unwrapped it and it was a tape, Charlie Rich's *Greatest Hits*. It was a good choice on Hilary's part. Some stars bring out albums of their greatest hits even when they've only ever had one or two—I mean, I don't object, I'd say that's good professional marketing, making the most of your assets—but that's not true in the case of Charlie Rich. He's had a number of big hits, the best known being "The Most Beautiful Girl in the World," but when I was just a kid I remember hearing "Another Place I Can't Go" and I couldn't get the tune out of my head. For years I thought it was the most wonderful song anyone had ever sung. I guess that's why Hilary bought it for me, she must've remembered, or it was serendipity. Anyway, I thanked her very much and told her there was no need for her to bring me a present. Then I say, "Uncle Bobby called in, with his new wife. Have you met her? She's Indian."

"No, I haven't, but, Michael, you mustn't say Indian," she said. "It's really offensive, it's racist. She's a Native American."

"Okay, okay," I said. "Anyway, they called in."

"And?"

"Well, they seemed happy enough together. He's selling guns."

Hilary frowned. "I'd heard," she said, giving me the impression she disapproved of anyone selling guns. She was in a critical mood, I could tell. "Uncle Vince says he probably picked her up in a bar. Was he sober?"

"Yeah, he seemed pretty sober."

She sniffed. "I guess he's been in rehab. Though how long it'll last . . . " Then she fixes me with her eyes. "Ever think of checking into rehab yourself?"

"What're you talking about, I've got no liquor problem," I say.

"No, but you're so fat, Michael. I can't believe how fat you're looking."

"I am fat," I say. "Sure I'm fat. What's the problem? It's not your problem."

"You're grotesque. Can you move anywhere?"

"I'm maybe not so good at running. I get people to run about for me, nowadays."

"Uh-huh. Can you move out of this room? Can you

148

walk? Can you stand on your own two legs or does that thing tip you over?"

"What thing?"

She indicated my stomach, my belly.

"Look," I said. "Most folk admire this."

"Uh-huh. They should have their brains examined. So ought you. And then what? Is this what your life's going to be? Lying here like this? For the rest of your life? People peering at you, and touching you?"

What have I done to deserve this? Worse than Hiram! "Hilary, no one in history's ever done anything like me before!"

"Your manager says, right?"

"It's true! Jesus! Who's ever been fat as me? No one." I look at her. I was suddenly angry. "What d'you mean, my manager? What d'you know about my manager? You been talking to Ma? Is this what this little call's about? Are you here for Ma?"

"Michael," she said gently. "Michael. Look, it's me, Hilary. Your sister. Yeah? I'm here as your sister. Sure I've been talking to Ma, what d'you expect?"

"She's welcome anytime she likes. The door's open."

"That's not what she feels." She smiles. "She misses you."

Then I felt sorry. "I'm sorry," I said. "I'm really pleased to see you. And I'd like to see Ma, if I didn't feel—" I stopped.

"What?" she asked.

"I don't know," I said. "But everyone else who comes

149

in here, they recognize me for what I am. They admire me. Then Ma comes in."

"Isn't that what mothers are for?" Hilary asked. "And elder sisters too, probably."

I said, "You're fat, too."

"Michael, I'm only two hundred and fifteen pounds. You weigh a thousand. You're a freak! You're a freak show!"

"What?"

"A freak show. Freak shows, Michael. They were all over the States in the last century. Dwarves. Bearded ladies. Harelips. Michael, you went to high school, you know what a freak show was."

"I don't weigh a thousand," I said. With some dignity, I may add. "I weigh only about eight hundred."

"Big deal," she said. "If you say so. All your promotional literature says you're a thousand."

I was going to tell her that was just marketing when she takes this folded piece of paper out of her handbag. She handed it to me, and I unfolded it. It was a magazine article. I won't say which magazine, but it had that glossy paper you get in magazines. The writer was one Lily Harper. Now, I could recall Lily Harper. She was a cute little redhead with nice legs who sat near me in the Shrine and asked me a string of soft questions. She was courteous and respectful, and I liked her. She couldn't've been more friendly. After half an hour or so she said good-bye and thanked me for giving of my time.

What she wrote—well, I've still got the article, but I

don't want to read it even now. It was pretty savage stuff. I'd read a few critical articles about me before, but they were always badly written and full of factual errors and cheap abuse. I'd never read anything like this. I guess I ought to read it to you, though I don't much want to.

This is it. It's pretty long, I may not read the whole thing.

"The Depravity of Fat" by Lily Harper. That was the title. "The Depravity of Fat."

"The Fattest Man" is the title of an exhibition drawn from the world of 19th-century America, in which every traveling circus had its sideshow of bearded ladies, dwarves and other physical and mental freaks. Much the most celebrated of such freak shows was attached to the Harry Kenton Circus, which toured the United States in the 1860s and early 1870s. Kenton was the son of an Episcopalian preacher, but he became a young entrepreneur of enormous energy. Among other achievements, he brought the first gorilla to North America in 1864. On August 15, 1864, a steel cage containing the beast was toured through the streets of New York like a captive general in the ancient Roman Empire, causing an immense sensation.

Kenton's Circus included performing elephants, baboons, lions, seals, and even a counting horse. Yet his freak shows were the centerpiece. In establishing them, he appears to have recruited within the primitive mental institutions and prison establishments of New York and Boston, and also within Native American communities.

151

Epileptics, failed suicides, murderers, rapists, polygamists and the mentally deranged were press-ganged into lining up alongside the usual troupe of hunchbacks, bearded ladies, dwarves, harelips and eunuchs. These unfortunates were treated by Kenton as virtual animals. Shackled by the hand or foot, they were forced to endure the curiosity and often abuse of the populace for long hours without adequate refreshment, and certainly without payment. Any of them rash enough to complain was punished either by whipping or starvation.

While liberals were offended, the crowds of North America flocked to see these specimens of degraded humanity, and Kenton became a wealthy man, who was to retire at the age of 35 to an estâte in Maryland (where he kept a private zoo).

Among Kenton's freaks was a black woman known as Rosa, who was billed as the Heaviest Woman in the World. Her advertised weight was 610 pounds. Very little is known about her, but she appears to have joined the freak show in 1870, and to have left by 1872, for reasons unknown.

"The Fattest Man," at Drake, Texas, is a direct descendant of the Kenton freak show. In a small wooden colonial-style house above the town lives the man who claims to be the fattest man in America. Visitors file into a dimly lit and sparsely furnished room known as the Shrine in order to witness a nightmare excess of wrinkled and tired flesh, to the tune of 1,000 pounds, sprawling on some beanbags shod in gold velvet. Brave souls may (on payment of an additional fee) approach "Mickey," this gargantuan monster, and touch his flesh.

I mean: "shod in gold velvet"! Shod. Sounds like a horse's hoof! Anyway, she went on:

More than 30,000 people each year pay good American dollars to witness this repellent sight. Why? The promotional literature on offer eschews all mention of freakishness, and instead advances the claim that "Mickey" is a work of avant-garde art. Says Hiram Cutler, promoter of the show: "This is the artist revealing his own body as art. This is in the great traditions of art dating back to the European Renaissance in the 14th and 15th centuries. Mickey is unique, in that no one has ever done anything like him before."

Anthropologist and art critic, David G. J. Wenger, of the University of Dallas, points out that our culture has arbitrarily chosen to value thinness above fatness. "'The Fattest Man'", he says, "disturbs and unsettles that perception." Moreover:

"What intrigues and challenges the visitor is the question: 'Is this real? Are my own eyes deceiving me?' The fat man known as 'Mickey' challenges and undermines our own notions of what it is to be truly human. Of course he is a freak, but his freakiness enables us to explore and maybe to rediscover the basis of our own humanity."

Many others disagree. They say that "The Fattest Man" is no more than prostitution thinly dressed up as art, and that it expresses the moral depravity of American consumerist society. In the opinion of leading cultural historian Reverend James Whitfield: "It's disgusting and degrading and a repellent spectacle. I find it personally appalling that anyone should wish to visit this place and still more allow impressionable young children to witness such a show. I don't regard it as an acceptable part of a civilized society."

One of the most interesting questions is whether Mickey himself has any conception of the exploitative nature of the undertaking in which he is engaged. Without doubt, he is exploiting his body for financial gain, yet one suspects that there is a degree to which he himself is being exploited . . .

I'll skip some of this.

No one could easily describe this experience as a pleasant one. The low lights and soft Buddhist music may attempt to disguise the ruinous physical condition of the 24-year-old man on his beanbags, but they are unable to mask the fetid and nauseating odor of his carcass, a reek which stays in the nostrils for hours and even days afterwards. This is the stench of decay and decomposition; indeed, it is also the stench of moral corruption. The truth is that "The Fattest Man" is an exhibition of staggering grossness and depravity, a throwback to the cheap inanity of Harry Kenton's freak shows—

And then it went on and on. That was it, this article by Lily Harper. Well, I read it through pretty quick, I confess. I couldn't get over how sweet and pleasant she'd made herself appear and then how unpleasant she'd managed to be in the article. Okay, that's what journalists do, and I'm sure she's got a great future ahead of her, but I did feel I'd been made a sucker. I handed the article back to Hilary.

"You keep it," she says, pushing my hand away. "You keep it."

"I don't want it. It's trash. Is that why you've come here?"

"Michael," she says.

"Is that the reason?"

"I thought you ought to know the kind of stuff that's being written about you. This isn't the only article. There are plenty of others saying the same."

I felt quite bitter. "Thank you, big sister."

She half gets up. "We haven't met in such a long while. I was hoping what they said, these articles, wasn't true. But it is. I mean—where is all this getting you to, Michael? Where are you heading?"

"I'm heading where the river takes me," I say.

"Oh, sure. What the heck does that mean? All that means is you don't know where you're going."

"It means I'm not trying to swim against the current," I tell her. "It means this is my business," I say. "This is my business. How else am I meant to make a living? Digging up dinosaur turds and getting paid for the privilege? What am I meant to do? I'm fat, Hilary. You haven't grasped what that means. I don't have your brains. I don't have Zoe's looks. I'm not an artist like Pa was. I'm fat! And that's it! If you're fat like me, you've got nothing except your fatness!" I was really cross. I quoted that saying to her: "If life gives you lemons, you make lemonade!"

She sat down again.

"Sure," she said softly. "Sure. Well . . . " She didn't say much for a moment. "Well, sure, if that's your decision, Michael. Honest, I'm not telling you how to live your life. I'm not trying to do that. I know what you mean about lemons. I just think you ought to know what's being said about you. And you do smell. You maybe don't notice it, but you smell awful. Honest, Michael. You stink dreadful. I wouldn't be saying this if it weren't true."

"If I smell, I smell no different from anyone else."

She shrugs. "Believe that if you like."

"If I smell, it's the smell of flesh. It's me. Who says it's an unpleasant smell? Jesus!"

I told her, if she'd come to preach at me I wasn't going to listen. Thanks for the tape, buddy, but I wanted to eat, I had food to get through. And I was running a business. I had folk outside waiting to see me. I was quite angry. So I just did, I went back to eating my meal. She sat and said nothing and then, in the middle, as I was eating, she got up and went away. Didn't say anything, just went. I was sorry about that.

When Hilary'd gone off I tried smelling myself. That's not so easy, it's like tickling yourself. You tickle yourself but it doesn't make you smile.

156

So I raise my arms to my nose and sniff. Well, sure, there is a smell. Who says it's an unpleasant smell? It's the smell of flesh, the smell of being alive, the smell of being human. People spray perfumes on themselves to shut it out, I reckon. They can't face up to being human, so they spray on extract of some other animal, like a civet.

I saw a civet once. A civet's a kind of small goldenish cat, and I saw one in the Houston Zoo. It was in a cage with a bit of dead tree. I was on a high school outing and we went to Houston by bus. It took hours and hours, in that bus. As I recall it, the civet was bigger than a domestic cat but not by so very much. It looked pretty unhappy, tell the truth, padding about in its cage with the dead tree branch thinking of the jungle or wherever its home was and ignoring the people looking in at it, entirely like it didn't even see them, like they didn't exist. I guess it was hungry, though I don't know. The floor was concrete. It was its eyes that upset me. My ma always says, the eyes are the window to the soul and the eyes of this civet . . . it looked crazy. I guess it's still there, padding up and down, waiting for something to happen, like that old-timer who used to live in the chicken shack, but I wouldn't go back to the zoo now. I don't hold with shutting dumb animals up in cages; it's a demeaning business.

★

I couldn't read the article again until the place had closed down for the day. I didn't want anyone to see me reading

157

it. Once everyone'd gone I unfolded it and read it again, right through. I read it several times, and I have to say it stung me. I don't know that I'm so very thin-skinned when it comes to criticism, but I kept thinking how Hilary would've talked about it to Ma, and maybe to Zoe too. That stung me. I showed it to Hiram Cutler next time I saw him, which was about four days later.

I should say I hadn't been seeing so much of him of late, he'd gotten involved in other business ventures. It didn't seem to me wholly professional of him, in my opinion, not with the tour coming up, and nor did I like the free and easy way he'd breeze in and light up a cigarette and pour himself some of my Scotch whiskey like it was his. He called the whiskey "wild mare's milk": "C'mon Colonel, let's have some of that wild mare's milk," he'd say, or, "Where're you hiding that wild mare's milk?"

This particular evening was just the same. He poured himself a full glass, and then he sat on the windowsill swinging his legs with the dusk behind him. It was warm weather as I recall, and we had the windows of the Shrine full open to get a bit of air.

I didn't show him the article at first. We talked about the tour and this and that.

"You eating well?" he said presently, with a look at me. "Keeping your weight up?"

"I'm eating normally, Hiram."

"Good," he said. "You don't want to fall behind. Not with this Douglas guy coming up on your tail."

"Why do all the leaflets say I'm a thousand pound when I'm not?"

He shrugged. "People like a good round number. I reckon we should put you up to one thousand one hundred. When were you last weighed?"

"Not for months."

"Let's get you weighed."

"I don't want to be weighed all the time," I said. "I'm not a prize bull."

He shot me a look. "A prize bull?"

"I need more respect."

"You bet you're not a bull, you're a hippo," he said. "You're a fucking prize hippopotamus."

"Hiram, I'd prefer it if, as my business manager, you could be here more often instead of shooting off to Mexico half the time."

He kept on swinging his legs and sitting on the window, and drinking my whiskey and looking pleased with himself. As always. It would've been good if he'd misjudged and gone over backwards out of the window, but he kept his balance.

"Okay, fat man," he said presently, after lighting a cigarette. "We'll keep you on a thousand for the moment. Who said I was in Mexico?"

"Maria."

"What she say?"

"She said you were in Mexico. Were you in Mexico?"

"Sure, I sometimes go to Mexico," he said. "It's not a federal crime, far as I'm aware, going to Mexico. What's the big problem? You're making good money. What's going on?"

"What about this?" I showed him the article. "Have you seen this? What does she mean, I'm engaged in prostitution? D'you reckon what I'm doing's prostitution?"

Hiram glanced at the article. He seemed quite pleased. "What's wrong with a little healthy prostitution?" he said. "Some prostitute their bodies, some prostitute their minds. Prostitution's just selling what you've got, ain't that so? It's making best use of your talents in order to earn a living wage."

"I don't happen to believe in prostitution. I don't believe in whoring."

He seemed to look curiously at me. "Well, if ya say so, Colonel. What's ya view on hypocrisy? Or should I say hippo-crisy?"

"What's that intended to mean?" I asked. "The woman who wrote that article, she's a hypocrite."

"And she's a prostitute," said Hiram. He began to walk round the room. "Mickey, everyone prostitutes themselves. You're prostituting yourself. Course you are. What else d'ya reckon ya doing? Selling your body for cash. Who isn't nowadays?"

"I'm not a prostitute. I'm a showman. I'm an entertainer. I live a decent life."

"That so?" He looked at me again, a superior kind of smile on his face. "Well, Mr. Showman," he said, "call it what you like. I don't mind. I won't split hairs with you."

160

I got angry with him then. "I'm not having anyone call me a prostitute."

"No. So what d'ya think Maria is then? She an entertainer too?"

"What d'you mean? What d'you mean?"

He looked at me again with that smile. "You may be dumb, fat man, but even you aren't that dumb. She doesn't come to you out of pleasure. Is that what you've been thinking? Jesus! That she comes to you for pleasure? Jesus wept! Maria's a whore, Mickey. Sure, she's a showman. And an entertainer. But she's also a whore who needs the money. Like you. Like me. Like the jerk who wrote this article. All whores. Like the rest of the world. Like the fucking President of the United States. Like the fucking Pope. Ain't no saints any longer, Mickey. We're all whores. This is America. I'm proud of it." He tossed his cigarette out the window. "The money to pay Maria comes out of the business. It's a business expense, old Denison knows all about it. There's no problem there. But if it'll make you feel holier that's fine by me, we won't hire her anymore. If that's what you want."

I lost my temper. I raised my voice and shouted at him to get the hell out.

He didn't move for a moment. Then he drains his whiskey and holds up his hands. "Well, I'll see ya in the morning. Have fun, Colonel."

I felt sick after that. I didn't want to think, I just wanted to eat and eat, to stuff my belly fuller than it had ever been. So I hauled myself into the cafeteria and ate anything

161

and everything I could find. Cold uncooked fries, cold burgers. Tins of beans. Anything and everything. Then I hauled myself back to my beanbags and lay there, bloated, bursting, heaving, watching my belly and waiting for the pains to begin.

Thing is, I'd known Maria was a whore. Sure I'd known. I'd pretended to myself she wasn't, that she liked me, she was my friend, but I'd known all along. She wasn't a real friend. Tell the truth, I didn't have any friends. All these folk from the other side of the world were writing me letters and taking my photographs and buying videos of me and Tiger, but none of them was friends. My only real friends were my cats and even then . . . I mean Lincoln wasn't a real friend. He didn't like being stroked that much, he still doesn't. He's a loner. There was just Tiger, good old Tiger. Out of the whole world, I had only one true friend, and that was a cat.

Thinking about this now, I see it differently to the way I saw it at the time. Looking at it now . . . well, I recognize being fat does make you significantly different to other people, and must hinder the easy development of friendships, but I also identify other factors. Anyone at the head of any business, responsible for employees and their welfare, is bound to feel somewhat isolated, however successful the business may be. That's inevitable. I also believe lack of friends is one of the downsides of being famous. That article talked about me being a freak: sure, I was a freak, not so much on account of my fatness as of my fame. Movie stars are freaks, pop stars are freaks, and being freaks, they're set apart. It's easy, in such circumstances, for tragedy to strike, but I didn't understand this until much later. At the time I just felt life was pretty unfair. I hadn't done anything wrong; I'd done my best. I was just unlucky, and I felt pretty bitter about it.

★

When she next came to me she'd been beaten again. Had this big yellow bruise on the side of her temple. You couldn't see it easily on account of her hair, but I saw it even so.

"Hi."

"Hi." I said.

She began to undress. She was silent. She was always very passive and silent.

I said: "Maria?" She looked at me. "I'm sorry," I said. "What happened? Who hit you?"

"It's nothing," she said.

"Let me see it," I said. I got her to pull her hair back. It was a real ugly bruise, quite swollen and yellow and purple. "Who hit you? I want to know," I say. "I'd like to know."

"Forget it," she says. She had this little leather skirt on, black leather, quite worn. You could see the wrinkles in the leather. And in her face. I mean it struck me, quite suddenly, she was already lining. She was so young but already she had these little lines round her mouth. The other thing that struck me, was how I knew nothing about her, beyond that she was Puerto Rican. I knew nothing else. And I kind of wondered, how many men did she go and service? How many a week? How many a day?

I say, "How much does Hiram pay you? For coming here? How much each time? How many dollars?"

She stiffened. "Thirty," she said.

"Thirty dollars? Why'd you do it?"

"I gotta live," she says simply.

That wasn't what I'd hoped she'd say. I'd hoped—I don't know what I'd hoped. But not that.

"I didn't know you were paid," I said, but I don't think she believed me. Why should she? She kept on undressing till she'd taken off all her clothes except for a bead necklace. It had wooden beads.

"If you don't want to stay you can go," I say.

She looked at me.

"You can go," I repeated. "It's okay. I'm easy. If you want."

She looked at me. She says in a very soft voice; "I need the money, Mickey. I gotta have the money."

I meant to send her away. I meant to send her away. I ought've done. But I'd been looking forward to seeing her so much and you know that saying, a stiff pecker knows no conscience. I guess that was it. Well, I'm not making excuses, I didn't send her away, I made her go through with it, as usual. It was a bad thing to do, I know; I'm not making excuses.

"I'm sorry," I said at the end, as she was dressing. "Please stay, will you? Just a little. I'll pay you to stay. I'll call up some food, we can sit and talk."

164

"What about?" she asked.

"Anything. I don't mind. Anything at all."

She didn't say anything.

"Please," I said. "I'll pay you. What would you like to eat? Pizza? Chili con carne? Donuts?" I was already moving to the phone.

She sighed. "I've got the cab waiting," and began to put on her clothes.

"I'll order up some donuts," I said. "Jackson's donuts. Have you tried them? They're top quality. They're the best donuts around. You should try them."

"Mickey, I can't." She seemed pretty subdued. "I've gotta go."

"Look," I said, "I'll pay you fifty dollars just to stay for an hour."

She stopped. She looked at me. "Just to stay?"

"Yeah. And I'll order up some donuts. You'll like them."

"Fifty dollars?"

"Yeah."

"Okay," she said. "I'll go and tell the cab driver."

So she put on her clothes and went out and told him, and I ordered up two bags of donuts. Then I went into my bedroom for the fifty dollars. Only I couldn't find them. I used to keep about five hundred dollars or so in a drawer and none of it was there. I couldn't understand why.

I didn't tell her, not at first. If I told her I thought she'd just walk out on me, so I kept quiet and kept her talking, asking her about Puerto Rico, and what Puerto Rico was

165

like and why she came here. "Mickey," she said, "what does it matter? Why're you interested? I came from Puerto Rico. I live in Drake."

"I'm curious," I said. Then I asked her where she lived in Drake. She said, "I'm sorry, I don't want to tell you. I live downtown."

"Was it a customer that hit you?"

"Oh, shit," she said.

"Was it Hiram?"

"Shit, Mickey, I don't want to answer this," she says, brushing a hand through her hair.

"Okay," I said. "Okay." By this time I was pretty sure it was Hiram.

I put on some music, any music, the first tape that came to hand. It turned out to be Hank Williams's "Your Cheatin' Heart," and I don't know it was the best of choices just then, I mean the words, they're kind of funny in hindsight, funny and sad, because Hank Williams died of a heart attack not long after recording the song. But maybe whatever I'd put on wouldn't've been right. I mean Maria just sits there, cross-legged, staring, with this bruise on her face, and then she covers her face with her hands and begins to weep. I hate seeing people weeping, I really do, I hate it. I said to her, "What's wrong? Maria?"

I shifted over and put a hand on her leg, to comfort her. But she recoiled and screamed, "Don't touch me! Don't touch me!"

I didn't know what to say. She went on weeping, like a child. In fact, that was what suddenly hit me, she was still a child. "How old are you?" I asked. "Maria, how old are you? Are you sixteen yet?" At that moment, she looked much younger—like thirteen even, or fifteen. She was so thin and scrawny. She didn't answer and I put the question again. "Maria? I need to know. Are you sixteen?"

"Yeah?"

"You're sixteen?"

"Why's it matter? Shit!"

"It matters because it matters!" I said. I was quite agitated. I mean, I thought maybe I'd been guilty of committing sexual relations with a minor. That's a serious offense.

"Yeah, I'm sixteen," she said.

I was relieved. Kind of relieved. Trouble was, I thought she was lying. She didn't look sixteen. At that moment, hunched up and weeping, she looked like a little child.

I felt sorry for her. I knew it was no good asking any more personal questions, but I did want to comfort her. And suddenly I thought how when I was upset, when I was a little kid, my ma always used to sit me on her knee in the parlor and tell me stories about the prairies and the buffalo and the first American settlers. I'd be sitting on her lap and leaning into her and feeling the softness of her body and the warmth of her breath on the back of my ear as she spoke . . . I used to love that, it felt so safe, like nothing could ever go wrong ever again. So I said to Maria: "Have you ever been to the Blue Falls?"

"Where?" she sniffed.

So I told her. She didn't seem to be listening at first, she just went on weeping quietly. But gradually she quietened, and I guess she was listening. I told her about walking up the dirt track, and crossing the railroad and walking through the scrub, and seeing the bluff, with these trees hanging out of the cracks and crevices. That's one of the more amazing things, these little trees which, tell the truth, aren't so little at all when you get up close, hanging out of the bare rock at weird angles. They're all gnarled and twisted, and you wonder how they survive, clinging on the rock. And then I said how you picked your way up the bluff and suddenly you got this roar, and saw the falls ahead of you, the river above the falls, like a sheet of rippling glass.

I hadn't ever told anyone else much about it, up to that point, and I don't know what she thought about it. She didn't ask any questions or anything. But it seemed to stop her from weeping, and as I went on she leaned forward and scooped up Tiger, and started stroking him, quite slowly, and even rubbed her cheek against his head, with her long hair falling forward. I could hear him purring very loud.

Then the donuts came. They were good, as they always are from Jackson's, but she was so taken up with the cat she hardly opened her bag. I urged her to eat, but she didn't seem at all hungry. Then there was the sound of a horn from outside and she put down her plate and stood up and said she needed to go. That extra hour'd gone already.

"Mickey, I'll be in trouble if I don't go," she says, "I'll get hit again. I've gotta go." And she asks for the fifty dollars.

"I'll give you it tomorrow," I said.

"Why," she says, "I need it now."

I didn't know what to do, so I went back in my bedroom and opened the drawer again where it was meant to be, but it hadn't been there an hour before and it wasn't likely to be there now. She came with me. "It was here," I said. "It's gone."

"That's no good to me."

I said, "Maria, I'm sorry, I don't know what happened to it. I don't have it. I'll pay you tomorrow."

She didn't believe me. She was really angry with me for wasting her time, she said, what did I think I was playing at, what kind of a jerk did I take her for? I kept saying I'd pay if she came back the next day, I promised. She said, "I'll be back, don't you worry."

Then she went. I felt pretty low, tell the truth. I shouldn't've made her go through it. I was just feeling pretty low and lonely, after Hilary and that article. That was how it happened. Maybe. I'm not looking for excuses. After she'd gone I listened to Hank Williams but it didn't do much good, didn't even touch the problem, and when I tried to stroke Tiger he just walked away. Like he was rejecting me. I don't know. Cats are curious intelligent creatures. Maybe it wasn't a rejection but that was how I interpreted it, at the time.

★

That article by Lily Harper was the first of I don't know how many. Before, I'd mostly had a favorable press, now every single piece seemed hostile. Like with sharks. They say as a general rule sharks won't attack human beings, but if there's a single particle of blood in the water they go crazy and tear you to shreds. Well, it was like that now with the press, they all piled in, slavering. Even the *Drake Chronicle*, which hitherto had always been on my side, ran a long article saying the Fattest Man show was seedy, immoral . . . that it damaged the town's reputation, attracted the wrong kind of tourists to what had always been a respectable neighborhood. Even quoting some pastor or church elder who called my house a bordello. And ended up by saying the kindest response to the degradation I offered was one of pity.

Other papers were much the same. I didn't read that much, I've never been a reader, and I can't recall it all word for word, but basically I was described as debauched and as purveying a cheap and tawdry spectacle. But I can't recall everything. What annoyed me most was when some guy wrote I was bringing the United States into disrepute. I was pretty stung by that. Because I'd always seen myself as a patriot running a successful business and contributing to the local and national economy, and enriching the culture too, and to be informed I was acting contrary to the interests of the country I loved . . . that's not a thing I could shrug off and forget. Think of it, this stuff was in print, it was being read by tens of thousands of people all over America.

At first I questioned the motivation of the people who'd written such material, and I contemplated taking some action to put them straight. But then I began to ask if some of their criticisms maybe weren't merited. I'd look at my belly, flopping off me, gray and slack and doubled by its reflection in the mirror, and I'd think of it in hostile terms, as an enemy that was taking me over, growing larger and larger, a cancerous tumor, or some giant parasitical beast that had dug its jaws into me with the sole aim of consuming, and that it would end up consuming me.

Hiram seemed to reckon any publicity was good publicity. That old maxim. How there's nothing worse than being ignored. And it's true these articles didn't seem to adversely affect the number of visitors we had coming through the doors. Numbers held up well. Sure, it was the school vacation time, numbers were always good then. But Hiram wasn't directly in the firing line, and when people came in and stared at me, when they pressed my flesh, when they studied the contours of my belly, when they made this or that personal remark, I felt literally exposed. What were they thinking? Were they thinking I was a prostitute? Where previously I had seen respect and curiosity on their faces, I now began to perceive what I interpreted as horror and distaste.

I tried blanking it away. Turning my back, keeping my eyes shut, listening to country music, pretending I wasn't where I was. Then I'd feel these fingers touching

171

me, stroking me, prodding me. Six hours a day I had to endure it. Lying in this little room, the Shrine. Staring at myself in the mirror. Being stared at. My self-confidence began to plummet fast.

The truth is you can't pretend like that all day, it'd drive you crazy, and that summer, in the end, I gave up showing the flesh. I wore some heavy velvet robes I had made up for me by a tailor in Drake. They pretty much covered me from my shoulders to my knees. The robes made me feel safer, as if they protected me from criticism, which I guess was an illusion; but that was how they made me feel. On the other hand Hiram didn't like them, and some visitors, who expected to see the flesh, were disappointed. From comments passed I know that some of them felt kind of cheated. Looking back, I reckon I was damned whatever I did . . . whether I showed the flesh or didn't show the flesh. I couldn't win.

That article, by Lily Harper . . . I guess if it had been only one article, I could've shrugged it off. Water off a duck's back. But it wasn't.

You see this TV crew showed up. I should've mentioned that: a Florida TV company was making a documentary about me. Hiram fixed it up as pre-publicity for the tour.

Chronology's important here. They first showed up in May of eighty-two, *before* Hilary's visit . . . *before*, if you like, my doubts set in. The director or chief producer, I don't know her exact job description, was a lady called Kim Duval . . . Katie Duval. I think it was Katie Duval. She was age thirty, I guess, and smart . . . she seemed very pleasant, and we got along fine, but I didn't pay too much attention to what she was saying. Then she went away, and I more or less forgot she'd ever been.

Months later, in the fall, *after* the Lily Harper article, *after* I'd started covering up, she came back with the TV crew. How many in the crew? Seven, eight, I couldn't say. They seemed to be everywhere, fixing up spotlights, setting up microphones, taping down cables, talking on phones, rearranging the furniture, smoking all the time. And barely speaking me a word. They'd be moving round me without saying a word, and one of them even trod on me. His shoe came down on a fold of my flesh and pressed it to the floorboards. He didn't apologize, maybe he didn't even notice, but as I've said, I do value respect. They had no respect for me. It was like I wasn't a human being, just another piece of furniture getting in the way.

Now, what I learnt was, they planned to be with me for a week. And all the time. *All* the time. In the morning when I woke, and in the evening when I hit the sack. When I was eating and drinking, and everything. Even when I was in the bathroom showering the cameras'd be rolling nonstop, even while I was sleeping. To give a complete picture of my life, that was the big idea of this documentary. That was what I'd apparently agreed to, or Hiram had agreed on my behalf!

Well, I was very unhappy. I couldn't recall having agreed to anything of the sort; if I had agreed, I hadn't understood what I was agreeing to. Everyone needs a certain degree of privacy. Eating's one thing. I kind of prefer to eat alone but I could just about have gone along with it.

173

But as for the cameramen being there when I was asleep, or in the bathroom . . . when I learnt that was what they intended, I felt it was a gross violation of my privacy.

I might've yet gone along with it if their manners'd been just a little more courteous. The point at which I cracked came as shooting was due to begin, with all the spotlights set up, when one of the camera crew asked me when I was going to remove my robe. So I told him that I wasn't removing it, I didn't remove it any longer. He looked kind of taken aback and went off to fetch Katie Duval. I then learnt that she not only wanted me to remove my robe, she also wanted me to take off my pants and put on a pair of black briefs. Black nylon briefs! She held them up, in a cheery kind of way. "As an experiment," she said.

I refused. There was all the stuff being written about me in the press, about licentiousness and depravity, and I refused. I did so politely but firmly; it was my right to refuse, or so I reckoned.

"Forgive me, Mickey, but you did agree to wear them," she said. "It was clearly understood. I remember talking it through with Hiram."

"He never mentioned it to me," I said.

"No? Well, I'm sorry about that. All we're asking is for you to try them on. You don't have to wear them all the time."

"But they won't fit," I said. Anyone could see that: there was no hope of them fitting me.

"Let's try," she said. "They'll stretch. Let's just try it

now." And she gives a nod to the cameramen to switch on the lights and start shooting.

Then I understood: she wanted to show me *not* getting into them. Failing to get into them. The idea being to mock me for being fat. Ho, ho, very droll. The indignities of a fat man's life. Or let's suppose, let's just suppose, for the sake of argument, I did succeed in pulling these things on. What then? This absurd black nylon tugged tight like a cord between my buttocks! Well, no ma'am. I wasn't playing ball with that. I'd put on a string vest for Eddie Dukes but that was years earlier and, besides, a string vest's nothing like a pair of black briefs.

I said to her, "You want an accurate picture of me, right? Well, the robe and the pants are what I wear. If you're aiming at a picture of me as I really am, that's what I should be wearing."

"You weren't wearing the robe when I came to see you before," she pointed out.

"That was different. I've covered up since then."

"Okay," she said. "But I assume, am I right, you don't wear the robe all the time? So long as we take some footage later, when you're not wearing it. For instance, when you're eating."

"Maybe," I said, "but I'm not wearing the briefs."

She seemed to relax. "Tell me, Mickey, do you ever actually, you know, wear nothing at all? I don't mean in the shower. I mean round the house, on warm nights."

"No," I said.

"Do you never just, you know, throw off your clothes?"

"No! I'm not having any naked shots."

"Okay, okay." She seemed disappointed. Then she said, "I can see this is kind of difficult for you. I mean, believe me, we don't want to make you do anything you don't want to. But we do want to give people an impression of your amazing fatness. We want to pay tribute to your fatness. It's a tribute documentary. Presumably you've no objection to us picturing you injecting yourself?"

"I don't inject myself," I said. "I don't inject myself with anything."

"Aren't you a diabetic?" she asks.

"Sure. But it's type two diabetes. There's no injecting." I could see she was even more disappointed at that.

"Okay," she said. "That's fine. Well, we'll just have to do the best we can. Okay?"

By this stage, though, I didn't feel like appearing in this documentary at all. I began laying down conditions. "I don't want the cameras in when I'm eating or sleeping, or in the bathroom. Those are private areas. And only when I've got a robe on."

"But Mickey, this is about your private life!" she said. "That's what it's meant to be. That's the deal."

"Sure," I said. "I understand. I'm sorry, but I'm quite a private person."

Well, at this she went off to confer while the camera crew hung about looking at me. I didn't like their attitude. I asked them to switch off the spotlights, which were generating a good deal of heat, and they did so but with an air of disrespect. "Boy, this is gonna be a party," said

176

one of them, and the other said, "This place needs fumigating." They looked at me. Next thing Hiram comes in the Shrine. "You guys go fix yourselves a coffee" he says and sends them out.

Once they're gone he crouches on his haunches. "Hey, Mickey, what's going on? C'mon. This is a big opportunity for you. This is the way to get big name recognition. What's the big deal? All they need is you to take off that stupid robe and put on a pair of briefs and eat some hot dog or pizza. Is that a lot to ask?"

"I'm not happy with it, Hiram," I said. "I know what they're doing. They want to mock me."

"Mock ya, hell!" he says. "Mock ya, hell. Ya too big to be mocked, Mickey. Ya the King of Fat." He punches me on the shoulder. "Get the robe off. I'll order up some pizza. What pizza you like best?"

"I'm not interested."

"C'mon! You're always claiming to be an entertainer. Let's see it, Mr. Showman. Why're you stuck on this Christ-awful robe all of a sudden?"

I said, "I don't want people looking at my belly. I prefer to be better clad."

"For Christ's sakes! You can't seriously be telling me you'll be wearing this Moslem blanket on tour! What's the game, fat man? Have you any idea how hard it is, getting a TV crew from Florida to Drake? Mickey? Have you any concept of that? Drake. What's Drake? Motherfuckin' Drake!" He sounded off about Drake for a minute or so, in a most unwarranted manner, how it was hick this and hick that, then a thought seemed to strike him. "You haven't got a medical problem under there, have you? Is that what's cooking under this robe?"

"I just happen to believe in privacy. I don't see why there should be cameras following me when I'm asleep. Or when I'm in the bathroom. That's my private business."

"You believe in privacy?" he laughed, not in a very pleasant fashion. "C'mon, fat man. Forget about the cameras, just do whatever you do every day. Shower, eat, sleep, doze, listen to your fucking country music, have a shit, forget they're here. What's the big deal?"

I told him I'd prefer him not to agree to things on my behalf without letting me know. He said, "Look, I'm your manager, aren't I? I'm your fucking manager. You need to trust me. And I'm telling you, if you want to be really famous, this is where it starts. Okay? So you chew it over. Okay?"

Then he went out and I was alone in the shrine. I lay there not moving, but my thoughts whirled in circles. I thought about all the things that had been written about me, how I was prostituting and degrading myself by putting on a freak show and bringing disrepute to Drake, and to America, and how the documentary would mock me and bring further criticism down upon my head. I thought about what Hilary had said, and Maria's bruises, and the way those dollars had vanished from my bedside drawer, and the black briefs, and the fact that they'd be here for a whole week. Then I thought maybe I was wrong. Maybe this documentary would end up okay, maybe it would help fat people in America, maybe it would make me much more famous. I could appreciate it wasn't entirely fair dragging a TV crew all the way from Florida if I was then going to send them back again without what they'd come to get. That seemed discourteous of me.

The truth was, I needed some independent advice. Not Hiram: he might tell me to trust him, but I didn't. I thought about Martha; what would she want me to do? I was longing to go on tour in order to meet up with her, because she'd more or less promised she'd get to see me when the show was on in Charleston, and I'd even begun to dream about her. Sexual dreams, full of flesh. The presumption, eh? When I'd never even spoken to her on the phone. But you can't control your dreams.

Well, I just went round and round in circles without being able to settle my mind one way or the other, and then Hiram came back in. "Okay?" He spoke in this light, pleasant voice, like I was some unruly child. "Let's go, shall we? Everyone's waiting."

"I'm not sure," I said. "I'm not ready."

"Oh, c'mon. Let's not play games. If we don't do it, it's all off."

"I'm not playing games. I want an assurance I'll be treated with respect."

"Ya do?" He stood and looked at me. Then he began to smile. It was a particular kind of smile, I didn't like it. It was the kind of smile like you might have trying to placate a kid who's in a tantrum by offering him a stick of candy. "Here. Here's what. Do what they want and I'll send Maria up. For the whole night. Okay? After they've gone. For the whole night. How's that for a deal?"

That decided me. The smile, as much as the mention of Maria. And his eyes. I recalled what my ma'd said, about eyes being the windows to the soul. It decided me. No, I said. No, no. Because at that moment I knew it must've been him that'd hit her. You know? I don't know how I knew, but I knew. No, I said. "I'm not doing it. I'm not going to Orlando either. I'm not going on tour. I'm closing the business down."

"What?"

"I'm closing it down, I'm calling it off. The whole business. I'm calling it off. You can send them back to Florida."

"You crazy or something?"

I wasn't going to talk it through with him. Suddenly I just wanted to be left alone in the house. It was my house. I built it, and I just didn't want these strangers filing through, looking at me, poking me, prodding me, inspecting me, talking about me. I didn't even want anyone to think about me. Not anymore.

I didn't want it. I'd had three years of it and I'd had enough. I'd had enough. I wanted out.

★

They say every smart businessman knows by a kind of intuition when to pull his chestnuts out of the fire. When to cut and run with clean heels. Like in the Wall Street crash. Like Randy McManus with his Burgerland

Experience. And maybe I have that intuition, and maybe not; maybe it's not intuition but luck, but that same day, after the TV crew'd gone, I had all the staff, the security, the catering manageress, the waitresses, the ticketing staff, into the shrine. I didn't go into detail, I just explained the show was closing early, and immediately, to the public, due to unforeseen circumstances. It would have been closed anyway from February, while I was on tour. The most tricky moment came when one of the guards asked when the show would be opening again, and then I had to say there were no plans for a reopening, and that left them all pretty stunned. You could see from their faces. I promised them three months' full pay and thanked them very much for their contributions, but I don't feel too good myself about how I handled the situation. I was feeling pretty emotional, tell the truth. Nothing seemed to be real. And I guess that was part of the wider picture, I'd got myself trapped in the show and forgotten the way off of the stage.

After speaking, I left them there and retired to the bedroom. I drew the curtains to. I couldn't believe what I'd done. After three years of hard work, just when the business was building up nicely, when I was on the brink of national celebrity, I'd packed it in. Suddenly I was scared. I remembered that old business maxim, it takes a good few steps to climb up a ladder but no time at all to fall off. I could recall the Reverend Candy, in Constant, saying how that was true not only with respect to business but also to the business of climbing the ladder up to Heaven, and at that precise moment I reckoned I'd just stepped straight off the ladder. It was a confusion on my part. What I didn't understand was that there were two ladders not necessarily the same. I'd maybe fallen off the ladder that led up to riches and fame, but it wasn't the same ladder that led up to God's Heavenly Kingdom.

But a panic seized me. How was I going to get by? What should I do? I was so heavy by this time I couldn't walk or even stand; my legs couldn't hold me upright and I had to haul myself along with my arms.

Maybe an hour went by, and I was still tormenting myself in the bedroom when Hiram burst in. He ranted at me for I don't know how long while I just lay there, stroking Tiger, and letting the abuse bounce off. Same old tactic I used at school, when the other kids shouted and taunted me. It always used to rile them and it did the same with Hiram. He became more and more wild, using language I prefer not to repeat on this tape, and when he got on to the subject of my family I felt such contempt for him I turned my back and put on my headphones. Then he started kicking me in the back. Not soft kicks but hard blows on my spine, and even with the music coming through the headphones I could hear the thud of each kick. I tolerated it for a while, being mostly concerned for Tiger, but when he turned his attentions to my head I reached out and grabbed his foot. My arms were still quite strong, and he couldn't pull loose. He stared at me, breathing heavily and hopping on his other leg, and I gave a twist and he fell over with his foot pinned under my belly. Then I began to roll over him. He started to shout. I could've rolled him flat if I'd wanted to, and I wanted him to know that, but at last I let him go and he stood back, panting and snarling. Then he grabbed my whiskey bottle and went out slamming the door.

A moment later he drove off. As the engine noise faded, I crawled from my beanbags to draw the curtains and let the daylight back in. The cloud of dust raised by his car was still settling. All Drake was below me, sunny in the afternoon. And I knew right away I'd done the right thing. If Hiram'd acted different, who knows? He might've persuaded me to reconsider. But every kick in my spine told me that my instinct had been correct.

The immediate future, however, was very difficult. I'd asked two or three of the staff to stay on for a few days to wind things down, and in those days I sold off all the shop merchandise except a few samples I kept as souvenirs, and I also went through the accounts with Mr. Denison. He came over from Tyler, and I learnt how I'd signed most of the profits away to Hiram. At least, there was my signature. Which I don't reckon I ever did sign, but sometimes I did put my name to papers without looking at them too closely. Isn't that what the famous do? Mr. Denison wasn't that helpful. I don't want to be critical but he kept pointing out in a dusty kind of way that it was my responsibility to read what I signed before signing. I told him I wasn't even sure if I had signed some of the documents; maybe some of the signatures were forgeries, but he reckoned there was nothing to be done.

Some weeks later, notwithstanding his advice, I took the matter to an attorney. He came from Austin, and spent an hour and a half with me. He was a polished operator, very charming. As I described the course of events he kept on raising his eyebrows in that sympathetic way attorneys do on the television, and when I gave him the documentation he leafed through it giving little whistles of surprise at the wickedness of human nature. Then I happened to mention how Hiram had kicked me in the back, and at this he made out he was really astonished. His mouth dropped open, his eyes widened. "How despicable!" he said. He wanted full details of the attack, how long it had lasted, how many blows had been landed, whether I'd put up any resistance, whether there were any independent witnesses and whether any photographs had been taken of my injuries. I said no to these last two points, which seemed to disappoint him, especially when I went on to say that being so well padded I hadn't been hurt that much. "You must have sustained considerable psychological damage?" he asked, and since he seemed to want me to agree, I agreed. So on we went, and at last he gave me his considered opinion that I had an excellent chance of success in the courts and that he'd be delighted to act on my behalf. He reckoned we—it was "we" by this time—ought to begin by claiming damages for what he called "traumatic injury and stress." Two million dollars might be an acceptable figure to be going on with, though naturally after negotiation one might end up accepting a slightly lower figure. "Sure," I said.

But we were in the ballpark of two million dollars. When he left we shook hands, and he took my hand in both of his hands and looked into my eyes and said: "We're going to win on this one. I'm really looking forward to working with you."

Well, he was just doing his job. He was delighted at the thought of all the money he'd be making out of me. But I didn't take it any further. Truth is, I was too scared Hiram might come back one night and do me some injury. That gun I bought off Uncle Bobby, the Beretta, I kept that near me for weeks and weeks, fingering it, just in case. But Hiram didn't come back, and I haven't seen him since that time. I guess he's either in jail or in Mexico, and I couldn't care which.

I got the phone numbers changed, and notified the tourist authorities about the show ending. I had the Fattest Man sign switched off and dismantled, and a notice put up, down by the highway: THE FATTEST MAN IN AMERICA SHOW HAS CLOSED PERMANENTLY. BEST WISHES. MICKEY. And then there came the time when the last member of staff left, and I woke up, one bright winter morning, alone, by myself.

So, you're asking, how did I get by? Well, first I pretended to myself I wasn't alone, and when that wore off I slept and slept, most of the time. Certain things kept me going, like the *Constant* "Country Hour" at seven p.m., I'd look forward to it all day. The D.J. was Teddy Montezuma and I used to pretend to myself he was a good friend. My only friend, in a way, except for Tiger.

Tiger was more of a comfort to me than I can say. He licked my skin a lot in those days, and sometimes I'd wake up and he'd be licking away like crazy. I guess it was the salt, but I took it for a kind of affection. But I was pretty far gone. What that article'd said about me being in a ruinous physical condition, it was true. I had a multitude of symptoms. I was thirsty all the time; however much I drank it seemed to make no difference. I was perpetually hungry even though I was stuffing my belly with dried rice, and sugar and cornstarch, and frozen peas, whatever came to hand. I was fatigued, so fatigued that if it hadn't been for thirst and hunger, I'd probably never have moved from my beanbags from one day to the next. And there were bed sores, constipation, tingling fingers, numbed feet, hemorrhoids, sweating fits. The worst of it was the vision. Suddenly I couldn't focus on objects properly, my eyes wouldn't hold them in focus. This new affliction was a great terror to me. My eyes had never troubled me before, but now I had to contemplate the possibility of going blind, and to consider what that might mean for my life, and whether life without sight would be worth hanging on to, and what would happen if Hiram came back and I was blind and at his mercy. I found such thoughts too painful and terrifying to contemplate and would try to put them from my mind, only to be reminded the next moment, when I saw myself in the mirror swimming in and out of focus. I know I should've called up a doctor, I know, it was pretty dumb of me, but I was too confused and scared. Whatever was happening to me I

186

didn't want to know about it, I just wanted to forget. And how did I forget? I forgot by eating and drinking, which made everything worse. I drank beer and beer and more beer, piling the cans up round me in walls like a castle, four deep, ten high, and when the walls got so tall they fell down I just lived in a sea of empty beer cans. My stomach pains were terrible. At times, hauling myself round the house like the snake in the Garden of Eden condemned to crawl on its belly for the rest of its days, I gave in to despair and lay crying to God, why did you make me fat? I am a citizen of the United States of America, I hold an American passport, why did you pile on the flesh and make me into something barely human? What did I do to offend you? Why didn't you make me ordinary, like other people? It was a black time. Since then Dr. Coughlan's told me I was pretty lucky one way or another I didn't die, or lose a limb, because apparently lots of people with untreated diabetes mellitus end up losing a leg or a foot or something. So looking back, I'm not reproaching God, I'm thanking Him for his great mercy.

I needed company. So I called up Maria. I'd got her number out of her and I called her, just to have someone to talk to. But, the thing is, she wouldn't talk to me at all. I knew it was her on the other end of the line but she pretended it was someone else. I said, "That's Maria, isn't it?"

"No," she said. I mean I know it was her.

I said, "It's Mickey here. I'd love to see you if you could manage it. Just to talk."

"No, she's not here any longer," she said, "she's gone away, she's left."

I said, "Where's she gone to?"

She said, "I don't know."

I said, "When she comes back could you tell her Mickey'd love to see her, just to talk, not for anything else. Please?"

She said, "I'm sorry, I know she's not planning on coming back. She's left Drake for good. She's finished with Drake."

"Maria," I said, "please. I'm sorry, Maria—"

Then she hung up on me.

I don't blame her, I didn't treat her with enough respect. I was always saying I wanted to be treated with respect but I didn't treat her with respect. I guess I had it coming to me a long way off. Even so, after that call I felt pretty low because I knew I didn't respect myself any longer, and I couldn't think who else to call. I could've called up my ma, and I nearly did, any amount of times. I'd lift the phone and dial all but the last number, I couldn't dial that last number. Who else could I have called up? Zoe was one. My little sister. She's not that little, she's twenty-four, but I think of her that way. I've always been closer to her than to Hilary. I mean Hilary always takes the serious angle on things, she's very judgmental. Quite preachy. Even watching comedies on the TV or something, she doesn't just watch, she picks holes in them here and there, she *analyzes* the characters. That's what she's like, whereas Zoe'll laugh at anything, even if it isn't that comic. She's got a lovely belly laugh. But I didn't call her up. If I did I guessed she'd tell Ma, and then things'd start getting even more complicated than they were anyway.

Solitude's a curious thing. Now, when I'm by myself, it doesn't matter to me at all. I know there are people out there who're thinking of me, just as I'm thinking of them, and I know that God's thinking of me too. But in those days I felt there was no one with me, and the solitude became like a force, pressurizing the walls of my mind. There were many times when I felt I'd made the wrong decision, when I reproached myself bitterly, though at other times I knew what I'd done was right. In hindsight, I guess I was still too proud. I was still puffed up with the pride of being the Fattest Man in the United States. I clung to that because it made me special, it made me unique. Even with my afflictions, I'd look down at my body and feel curiously awed by it. Those great sagging breasts, and the mound of my stomach, and the folds of interlapping flesh, fold on fold. It was my life's work. Okay, the business was closed, but I was still no less special. I might reproach God for not making me more ordinary, but the truth was, at that time, I didn't want to be ordinary.

Moving on. One night in the spring of eighty-three, when I ought've been on tour in Orlando or Charleston. I put in my usual pizza order, and presently I hear the motorbike climbing the hill. The bike stops. There are two pizza delivery guys, one a white guy covered in pimples he's tried to mask by growing a kind of fuzzy beard that doesn't work and the other a black guy who must be way over six and a half feet high. He can't even get in the door without clipping his head. That's something I've noticed in general about the American population, folk are getting taller and they're also getting heavier, or fatter, if you like. The boundaries are expanding steadily. Like with sporting records, every year or so someone runs faster or jumps higher or further.

This time it's the fuzzy-face. He gives me my pizzas and then, casually, as I'm paying, he says: "Hey! Mickey? Did ya watch ABC on Tuesday?"

"Yeah?"

"'Bout this fat guy in Oklahoma?"

I didn't know what the hell he was talking about.

"This guy in Oklahoma," he says. "Oklahoma City. Did ya see him? Ya've been overtaken!"

"What?" I say.

"Ya've been overtaken. This guy's one thousand and forty-two pounds! Didn't ya see him? On the evening news slot."

Above the beard his pimply skin shines in the moonlight, it looks kind of like the pitted surface of the moon. "Yeah?"

"Sure! He weighs one thousand and forty-two! I saw a picture of him on ABC on Tuesday!"

I reckoned the pizza guy was slinging a line, spinning a line I ought to say, making it up, but no, no, honest Injun, yes sir. Yes Mickey. No kidding. One thousand and forty-two. Hadn't told anyone for years, kept his light under the proverbial bushel. And then he lets me know I'm not even the second heaviest. That is, I'm the second fattest man, but there's a woman someplace on the West Coast like San Diego who is in the thousand region.

"What d'ya know?" says the pizza guy. "Ya got competition. Okay Mickey? Good eating!"

That's what I mean about business intuition. Or luck, sure. If I hadn't closed down the business, that news would've probably meant I'd've been forced to. I mean, third heaviest person in the States, it wouldn't carry the same appeal.

And yet I was mortified. To find I'd been overtaken! You see, money never was my great ambition. What I'd been striving for was celebrity, fame. I wanted to be famous. No one in my family'd ever been famous, not even a little famous. No one in Drake or Constant had ever been famous. That's what I'd wanted . . . to be someone beyond the ordinary, not part of the herd. To be someone that mattered. To matter, to make my life matter, to leave a mark on the world. I'd wanted it so much. Now I knew I not only wasn't famous, I wasn't even important, I was no one.

I didn't want to admit it, not for a long time, there was too much pain. But, speaking of what matters in life, I gradually came to recognize that somehow along the trail I'd lost touch with things that truly mattered. I hadn't only lost touch with my mother, my sisters, my family, I'd also lost touch with my own self, and I'd also lost touch with God. I never gave Him a thought from one week to the next. And in consequence my spirit was dying within me.

I've talked about it with Martha a little. We've discussed

it, the human spirit. What Martha says is it's like a candle flame, burning inside of each one of our bodies, and we've all got it, sitting inside us. And what we're here for, our task on this earth, is to protect that flame. We are keepers of the flame, Martha says. We have to keep that flame burning, protecting it from the wind, raising it higher and higher. That's all we're here for, in the end.

6

The tornado hit in May eighty-three, May eighteen to be exact, and changed my life for ever. I'm not going to say too much about it in general as it's common knowledge, it wouldn't help your project. All I will say is tornadoes are ranked from categories one to five on the basis of their destructive power, on the Fujita Scale, and this was category F-four. It ripped right through this area and caused major damage to property and person. Ten individuals died and there were hundreds hospitalized. As a kid I'd once or twice seen tornadoes from afar, like g snaky ropes hanging out of dark clouds on the horizon, like the trunks of elephants, and I'd been told how dangerous they could be if you were in their path, but I never truly comprehended their power.

You could say it wasn't entirely unexpected. Drake lies toward the south of what I believe's known as Tornado Alley, stretching right up through northern Texas into Oklahoma and Kansas, and there are little tornadoes every year in the spring and early summer. They generally fizzle out quickly enough, but a few get going and work up steam, and then they just carve along on a path of their own choosing, sometimes more or less straight, sometimes in a curve. They generally come from the south-west, but their precise path isn't predictable and there's no one yet's devised anything to control them. Tell the truth, I don't reckon anyone ever will. If they're out in open country it doesn't matter so much, but they're dangerous creatures. This was the worst tornado to hit Drake for years and years, and if it was only an F-four I can't imagine what a category F-five might be like.

It built over three or four days. It built and built. The weather was blustery. I knew something was coming even before there was much to see in the skies, because as air pressure falls I find breathing's more difficult, I wheeze in my chest. But I didn't take any precautions. I guessed it'd just be another big electrical storm, and for a long time I didn't even trouble myself to look out the windows, which might've alerted me to what was to come. However, even if I had looked out earlier, even if I had concluded a killer tornado was heading in this direction, I don't reckon I'd've done anything else. For one thing, I reckoned that the house being on the side of a hill any tornado would pass by, slipping into the valley below; for another, I just did not believe I could be caught in a tornado, I reckoned it was impossible. That's maybe why I'd never bothered to build myself a storm cave. You also have to recall my physical and mental state at the time, following the end of the business. I'd been spending my days lying in my bedroom doing nothing at all, just piling up the cans of beer.

The point at which I began to comprehend what was

happening was toward early evening on the eighteenth. The cats were restless, padding to and fro, and one of them miaowed—I guess it was Lincoln—to be let out. So I opened the door. Now, a strong, gusty wind was blowing and there was plenty of electrical activity, lightning flashes and thunderclaps, but what caught my attention immediately was the weird condition of the sky, particularly to the southwest, to the other side of Drake. I'd never, ever, seen clouds like it. Never. I'd always studied clouds with some interest, ever since I went fishing with my pa on Lake Constant, but I'd never seen clouds like these. At first I wasn't sure it wasn't some new malfunction of my eyesight. I mean some of them seemed like dark smoke from some garbage tip and some were almost pale and some were kind of dark sludge green, but it wasn't just the colors, it was their behavior. They were whirling round in different directions, and much faster than they ought've been. That's the effect of the vortex of the storm, I know that now, but at the time my mind was dull, slow, inert, and I couldn't make out what was happening. All I could do was rub my eyes and stare. One of the strangest things I also became aware of, and I can't easily explain this, was that the sky to the northeast was also in a state of profound disarray. I watched for some time, first looking this way, then that, and all the time the sky to the southwest was getting darker and darker, and the little greenish clouds suddenly weren't so visible, they seemed to have been swallowed up by this huge black cloud. Black as night, blacker. And round the edges of it were specks of dark matter, and I suddenly realized these were pieces of debris cascading through space, and that was when I knew, for the first time, I had to be looking at a tornado. I didn't quite believe it, even then. I thought all tornadoes looked pretty much the same, with a sharply defined funnel like the trunk of an elephant, and this didn't seem to have a funnel. No one'd told me a tornado funnel could be half a mile wide. Then I felt the air sweeping toward me and heard a howling sound.

If a tornado's heading your way it makes good sense to take evasive action. You get in the car and get the hell out fast as you can, and if you haven't got no car or any other motorized transport you run. Get below ground, if you can. Well, none of those options was available to me. I had no car and I couldn't run; couldn't really walk, either. And, as I say, I had no storm cave. I looked round for the cats, and I managed to grab Tiger. Lincoln was racing off across the parking lot and I had no chance of reaching him. By this time the howl was more of a roar, like the roar of a freight train coming through a tunnel but louder, and the darkness seemed to be rising above me, and I knew I had only a few seconds left before it hit.

I did get back inside the house, and I hunkered down, waiting. Tiger was terrified, and struggling so much I reckoned I might lose him. I was putting him under my robe next to my belly when the tornado struck. I can't describe it, if you've never experienced a tornado, I can't begin to describe it. It was like nothing on earth—darkness and confusion, the clattering and battering of innumerable objects, the roaring of the mighty whirlwind. I couldn't see what was happening, I didn't dare look, but it sounded like the entire house was being torn apart. In my terror I clung to the floor, trying to hide where there was no place to hide and expecting any moment to be struck by some deadly object, when something else happened: I was lifted up, raised. All eight hundred pound of flesh of me was swept outside clean off the ground and taken into the vortex, where I spun up and up like a feather till I seemed to stop and rest on the billows of the air, in an area of calm, like the palm of God's hand. Like God couldn't decide what to do with me, whether to take me up further or let me fall, like He was weighing me in the balance of His great judgment. I've never spoken with too many people about it, but those I have talked to always ask how high I was off the ground and I answer maybe thirty feet or fifty feet, and how long I was in the air and I answer maybe thirty seconds or fifty seconds. The true answers are I don't rightly know. I do know that my progress upward, as I spun round and round, seemed very very slow, and that at last I reached an area where time had entirely stopped, or that was my impression, and that there I was held suspended, feeling the eye of Providence upon me, and with the wild air billowing round, for what seemed like all eternity. Then I was let fall, and I fell swiftly to the ground. I landed heavily, not knowing where I was, not sure if I was dead or alive; the impact knocked all sense out of me and I guess I was unconscious for a certain period. It also busted my right arm in four places, and three rib bones, though I didn't realize that at first. My immediate concern when I came to my senses, when I found I was still alive, was with the quantity of stray debris whirling through the air on the coat tails of the tornado. Nothing hit me, but I was real lucky, because a moment later I heard a massive crash of something metallic landing nearby. Later I discovered it was an upended Buick truck, flown some half a mile, landing in the parking lot. If it'd landed on me I'd've been finished.

Excuse me. I need a drink.

Let me resume. Even after the tornado'd swept on it wasn't safe to move. There were bolts of lightning shooting through the air and colossal claps of thunder, followed by a bombardment of rain and hail. This rain was like spears, driving at the horizontal, and the hailstones were big as those hailstones I told you about when I was at the Ranelagh Grand. I prayed for forgiveness and deliverance, recalling my ma and pa and my sisters and my many sins, and also thinking about my two cats, Tiger and Lincoln. That storm went on for hours. The lightning flashes gave me glimpses of the devastation, but only as daybreak arrived, dark and heavy, was I able to see the true nature of the damage. My house was still upright, and some walls were standing, teetering, unsupported; but the roof was gone, and there wasn't a pane of glass not broken, and most of the contents—chairs, tables, everything—had been sucked out and carried away. The cafeteria was in ruins, the emporium had disappeared like it'd never existed, and the palms had all sheared off at the trunks like some jagged blade had gone through them. There was no sign of either cat, and tell the truth I had no hope for them. As for me, my body was aching all over, my arm was beginning to hurt bad, and I had stabbing pains in my ribs; I was cut all over from shards of flying glass, and I was drenched through. Yet I was alive. I felt like the survivor of a shipwreck, tossed by the seas onto the safety of land, and I began to shed tears, thanking Providence for the warning that I had been served.

I saw the only way I was going to be able to raise assistance was by my own strength of will. I couldn't walk but I could crawl, and that's what I did. I crawled and hauled my body down the hillside, under the dark sky, till I reached the silent highway. There I waited. Drake was below, all gray and quiet. There seemed no cars coming or going anywhere, and since I was very weary I presently let the weight of my belly drag me down and I lay me down on my good side, though it was still raining and the asphalt was swimming in wet gray mud draining off of the hillside, and I rested the side of my head on my good arm. The water was running under me, it was like lying on the bed of a river except the river was concrete. So I waited for help, and as I waited I again prayed to God in His great mercy. Then I began to ask myself if I didn't need to get someplace else, because I knew of a house about half a mile down along the highway, and I hauled myself to my knees and began to crawl further that way, panting and groaning, sobbing and gasping, getting more and more exhausted. When at last I got to the house, which was another wooden place like mine, I found nothing but an upended, broken-backed piano.

The damage caused by a tornado's generally well defined. You get a single swath of destruction that's maybe two hundred yards or two thousand yards wide. Within that swath there's major devastation but outside it, even a few yards outside, there's no damage at all. That's not always the case, you may get a kind of family of tornadoes, with a main vortex and several satellites that spin around it, but that's the general rule. And it was the case here. Suddenly I was out of it, beyond, and in the clear. There were trees and shrubs still standing. Houses untouched. Even a bird singing. It was a sweet sound, like a stream of silver, and it kind of gave me fresh encouragement. I crawled on down the hill, till at last I saw a greenish station wagon driving along and the sight of it filled me with hope, and I waited as it wound up the hill toward me, very slowly or so it seemed to me, till it was near enough for me to hail. It stopped. I didn't know then, I only found out later at the hospital, what I looked like: dripping with slime and blood, my face swollen from the hailstones. I must've looked barely human. The guy inside the station wagon was shocked to see me; I guess he was shocked to see me alive at all. But he knew me, it turned out. "Jesus! Jesus Christ! Ya the fat man! Ya Mickey!" He'd been to see me, a long while back, with his family.

Squeezing into the station wagon was the worst of it all. I couldn't fit in the front and had to get in the back, which was full of machine parts; he was some kind of engineer, I guess. He kept saying, "Christ knows if the suspension's gonna take this. Christ knows." Once I was in he slammed shut the doors and inspected the undercarriage. He said: "We've got about zero clearance, Mickey." He drove down pretty slowly, I can tell you, every so often the undercarriage scraping the metal of the highway. It was real good of him. He drove me to the hospital. It was full of folk cut and scratched about and dazed, and a number seriously injured, including a little girl with a gash in her forehead, and we had to wait for I don't know . . . hours. But everybody seemed kind of happy. That must seem a strange thing to say, because we knew lives must've been lost. One guy'd even seen a couple of bodies. But everyone was friendly, talking about what'd happened to them. They asked about me but I didn't say a word about being lifted into the vortex, I just kept real quiet, reckoning they'd probably think I was inventing it all. Bragging. I mean it's not something I've ever talked about too much. Being carried up into the whirlwind? Being transported, light as a feather, a full seventy-five yards? Yeah, sure; who ya kidding? And then ya woke up, huh? So I just sat on the floor and listened to the conversation going on round. No one seemed to pay me too much attention: I was just another patient, waiting in line. Just another American.

And it was . . . it was real nice. The atmosphere was very warm and homely, almost like being back home in Constant. We had blankets wrapped round, to warm us up, and everyone was friendly, so friendly, I felt like weeping. I really did. I hadn't been with ordinary folk for so long and I'd forgotten what it was like, just being with them, not being special. I mean, it's hard to express, but for the first time in years I felt ordinary again, and I didn't mind.

★

I now draw near the final part of my story. I may fit it on this tape, I may not. I'll try keeping it tight as possible.

After the tornado, while the house was being rebuilt, I stayed in the Best Western, courtesy of my insurance company. It was kind of enjoyable, better service than I might've expected from a two-star hotel. There was a surprise for me when I checked in, because Chuck Watson was standing behind the front desk. He didn't tell me exactly why he'd left the Ranelagh Grand, his sole comment being that it only took one straw to break the camel's back, but I guess that referred to the perpetual stream of petty complaints directed towards him by Mr. Saker. It was good meeting up with him again, and chatting about old times. My room was small but comfortable enough, once the bed frame had been moved out and some beanbags moved in; it had a TV and it was near enough to the coffee shop, which turned out to be first-class, particularly in the pastry department. I'd sometimes drag myself in there but I didn't want to embarrass other customers, and most of the time I used room service. I was glad to, I had a lot of hard thinking to do. There was a Gideon Bible in the bedside drawer, and as I began to study it in earnest I came upon lines in the Book of Nahum, chapter one, verse three, stating how the Lord hath his way in the whirlwind and in the storm, and I recalled the preaching of the Reverend Candy, who had spoken about the last trump when the quick and the dead would be raised to eternal life, bursting upward in the twinkling of an eye. In this way I was led to understand what had happened to me in the tornado, why I had been lifted and spun through the darkness, for when the Lord let me down from the vortex He was telling me I was not yet fit to be received into His Kingdom. I saw I needed to change the direction of my life, to cease hankering after fame, and to set my spiritual affairs in order.

It was out of these reflections that I wrote to my ma, and next thing I knew she'd shown up. Three long years had passed since I'd seen her last and she looked much older. Her hair was quite gray and silvery, and there was a paperiness to her skin. I was shocked; it was the first time I'd ever thought of her as old, and I felt a tightening round my heart.

We had plenty to talk about, as you may imagine. She said how pleased she was to receive my letter, because she'd heard of the tornado on Constant County Radio and had been worried sick whether I was safe. So I told about me being taken into the whirlwind and that I interpreted it as a warning. She said: "A warning? What makes you so darn sure it was any kind of warning?"

I quoted her from Nahum: "The Lord has His way in the whirlwind and in the storm, and the clouds are the dust of his feet."

She was pretty surprised at me quoting the Bible like that—"I never knew you were such a student of religion, what's happened?" I told her nothing'd happened, I'd just been doing a spot of thinking, and she says, "Now that can be a dangerous thing to do, thinking too much—you ought to take care." That's the kind of thing she always says. Finally I did manage to bring out what I wanted to say, that I was sorry what had happened and that she'd been dead right about Hiram Cutler. She laughed: "Aw, Michael, I was jealous. You know? It was darn stupid of me. A man's got to stand on his own two feet. He can't have his ma holding his hand all his life."

Family's family. We were both pretty emotional, I guess. The ties of flesh and blood can't be sundered. I called up some iced tea and cheesecake and we had a long talk about everything, and she gave me an update on all the news. She told me Zoe was dating this guy in Tyler who was a mountaineer. Zoe! My little baby sister! I couldn't believe my ears! But it was true, it still is. His name's Robert Brain and he's a world-class mountaineer, he's almost famous, in the American mountaineering world. Ma said, "There's Zoe, and Hilary, and you, and I'm proud of the lot of you. Whatever and whatever and whatever. It makes no difference." She also gave me the latest on Uncle Bobby and Anya, his Indian wife. Not in too much detail but she said she understood from various hints Anya'd dropped that not only was Bobby back on the liquor but there were money problems. She shook her head: "Every family's got its black sheep." I was kind of pleased by that, because I'd been afraid she thought of me as the black sheep.

One thing she was pretty concerned about was my physical condition; as I may've told you, she has diabetes mellitus herself, and when I told her some of my symptoms, notably the numbness in my feet and my weird eyesight, she called a doctor up straight off. "I'm not hearing another word out of you until you've seen a doctor," she said. "You're a darn fool if ever there was one." When I told her I didn't want any doctors she gave me quite a talking-to about my responsibilities because, she says, no one lives just for themselves; if something happens to me, she says, all the family's affected. It was just like I was still a kid. I was pretty relieved, tell the truth, after she'd made the call. When I'd been back to the hospital to have my broken arm seen to I'd nearly asked the doctors myself, but I was too scared of hearing bad news.

The doctor I went to see was Dr. Coughlan, at the St. Theresa of Avila Clinic. It's a Roman Catholic clinic and there's this big portrait of the Virgin Mary and the Infant Jesus hanging in the foyer, with the Statue of Liberty in the background. I liked Dr. Coughlan as soon as I saw him. He did various tests on me and gave me medication to make my pancreas create more insulin; he also told me about the dangers of inadequate circulation and how I needed to do some gentle exercising, and if my vision failed to improve or if the numbness in my legs got any worse I ought to contact him immediately. He did talk to me about weight reduction, but without trying to scare me, and I was grateful for that. I mentioned the idea of stapling the stomach and he said no, that wasn't always necessary, or even the best option, it was perfectly possible to reduce the size of my stomach some other way, if I wanted to go down that road. I mean he's a pleasant guy, I've never felt he's judging me or criticizing or threatening, not like that Dr. Griffith I was telling you about at the San Antonio Clinic. Even after that initial consultation I felt better, almost at once, maybe on account of knowing I was in the care of a good physician. Since then my health's improved pretty steadily. My vision's picked up, the tingling's gone in my feet and fingers at least most of the time, I don't sweat so much, and I'm not nearly so tired. But maybe there's other reasons to explain all of this.

Before moving on I should tell you about the cats. My assumption was they'd both been killed in the storm, but Lincoln survived. I finally caught up with him, two or three weeks after the tornado, when I was paying a visit to the ruins of my home. I'd got a truck driver known to Mr. Watson to transport me up the hill, and as I got out of the truck Lincoln wandered up affectionate as anything. He'd been living wild and he was skinny but in good enough shape. Old Tiger had passed on, however. He was with me under my robe when the tornado struck but he must've slipped from me within the vortex, and I found his body, or what remained of it, near the wreckage of the cafeteria. I guess he died from the impact of the fall, or maybe he was hit by some lump of debris. I mean there was debris scattered all over the hillside, chiefly chunks of wood but also sheet metal asbestos and even that piano I mentioned. Some surprising things survived intact, including a filing cabinet complete with contents, and a chair made by my pa. I told you about it: it's the one with the armadillo on the back, and I found it two hundred yards away in the tumbleweed, unharmed. Not even a scratch. But Tiger was out of luck. He was always a very careful cat about his appearance, always washing himself, not like Lincoln, and it made me break up to see his beautiful white fur covered in dust and flies swarming round the body. Folk say a cat's only a cat but he was a good friend to me. That's one thing about animals I'd like to say: If they're friends, they don't lay down conditions about the friendship. They don't judge you except by how you behave towards them, they don't judge you for being fat. I'd like to believe cats and other animals go to Heaven but there's nothing along those lines in the Bible. I know, having looked. On the other hand, there's nothing I'm aware of in the Bible to say animals don't go to Heaven, and maybe they do. If I was constructing a heaven, I know I'd have a cat like Tiger right there.

I buried him myself. Seems incredible, doesn't it, but I did, even though I'd only one good arm. Somehow, I was able to crouch, and walk . . . not really, but shuffle walk, on all fours. As if I'd gotten new strength. And I took his body to a little patch of ground to the side of the parking lot and scratched out a hole with a piece of metal. The ground was still soft as anything after the rain and I made a good hole and buried him safe from those flies.

The rebuilding of my house took less than two months, and by late summer I was back home. I didn't rebuild the cafeteria or the emporium, there was no point any longer. I got in new furniture, carpets, kitchen appliances. I had the Texas palms replanted and another white picket fence put up, just like before. Everything was covered by the insurance, which was a relief. Ma helped. She used to come down every week or two, help with the general house-keeping. I liked her coming but I felt kind of guilty about it too. Every time she'd bring along with her a copy of the *Constant Bulletin*, and while she was cleaning up or cooking or seeing to my laundry I used to look through the real estate pages thinking maybe I ought to move back to Constant, that Constant was my real home. I reasoned that it would save her the trip, particularly as she was getting older, but when I said as much she was quite offended. "I'm not old, Michael! I'm only fifty-four!" And when I said I might move back to Constant she seemed kind of put out, she said, "You can't move back to the past, Michael. The past's dead and gone."

One day she was puffing up my beanbags when she came upon some shots of Martha I'd pinned in my bedroom, on the wall. They'd survived the tornado inside the filing cabinet, and among them was that photograph of Martha posing as a gunslinger. "And who might this fine young cowgirl be?" Ma asked. "Or is it none of my darn business?" Well, I told her—maybe blushing very slightly, though she pretended not to notice—I told her, just a fan, which is all Martha was at that point, and tell the truth I didn't know if she was even that any longer. After pulling out of the tour I guess I felt I'd let her down, and for months I hadn't even had the courage to write to her. It was all mixed up in my mind with Maria and how I'd not behaved well as I should've. Then, after the tornado, when I was staying in the Best Western, I'd written—on hotel notepaper—but I'm not so good at that kind of letter, and since I hadn't received any reply I guess I thought, well, that was it. It was only ever a kind of dream. What can you tell about anything much from a letter?

But then, late one morning in the early fall, imagine me dozing on my beanbags, nothing's happening, all's quiet, the TV's showing ice hockey or baseball or something, a cab drives up and the driver hands me a letter. "Personal delivery, Mickey," he says, and drives away.

I open it. It's on Best Western notepaper, the same I'd used when writing to her. And the same address: the Best Western on Cramer. In Drake! What it says is pretty simple:

Dear Michael,
Chance brings me to Drake on the way to Fort Worth. If you care to give me a call, I'll be waiting.

Yours very truly,

Martha (Watts)
P.S. I've been trying to call you, but your number's changed.

I couldn't believe it. I'd kind of assumed she was no longer interested in me, since she hadn't written, and as for her being here in Drake, I couldn't take it in. I went to the telephone. "Michael? Is that you?" she says, before I'd said a word, when she picked it up.

I'd never heard her voice before. It was a warm southern voice, quite deep and throaty. Deeper than mine. Remember: I'm *reedy*. I'm *squeaky*. The fat guy with the squeaky voice.

"How long're you here for?" I asked.

"Just a day," she said, "I happen to be passing this way, I'm on my way to Fort Worth, so I thought I'd give you a call. I'm sorry about it closing down."

"If it hadn't closed down it would've been torn away by the tornado," I said.

She got a cab, brought her up the hill.

Meeting Martha was—what shall I say? We met. Yeah, we met, at long last. Was she like in her photos? Yeah, I guess. No, I guess. She was taller. She was fatter. And she was more beautiful than I guess I could have imagined.

I don't rightly know what she thought of me, you'd have to ask her. I was pretty self-conscious. I was also pretty embarrassed, for one good reason. Two good reasons, tell the truth. First was that, as I say, I felt I'd kind of let her down by not being in Charleston as I'd promised. The second reason—I'll tell you the second reason. I've told Martha, so I'm not embarrassed any longer. The cab driver who'd brought her up the hill was the same cab driver that used to bring up Maria and Naomi and the other girls. And I didn't know what he might've said. Probably he hadn't said anything, but I didn't know for sure. But Martha was pretty nervous too, in fact, she was slightly breathless, like she'd walked up instead of coming by cab. First she made out like it was just chance she

210

happened to have been traveling through Drake, that she was going to see someone she knew in Fort Worth. I said, "When are you seeing him?" (I don't know why I assumed it was him.)

She said, "Oh, it's a kind of open invitation, that's all. It don't matter too much." She said he was an old friend of her family. "I guess I'll move on tomorrow," she said. "I'm kind of expected tomorrow, that's when he's expecting me, but it don't matter too much. It's an open invitation."

She came in and the place was looking spick-and-span, which was a relief, because my ma'd been cleaning round the day before. I made her coffee and cookies, and introduced her to Lincoln, who's never liked strangers as a general rule. You'd've thought when so many visitors were coming through the doors he'd've got accustomed, but not so; he's still pretty standoffish. He likes a certain respect. But he liked Martha. Anyway we had our coffee and cookies, and then I showed her the distorting mirrors. All the mirrors used in "The Fattest Man" had been smashed but I'd bought new ones. I don't know why exactly: I guess because I liked being able to see myself squeezed thin, almost normal. But when Martha saw me in that mirror she said oh no, I looked much better as I was. She laughed. "You look goofy all thin!" It was good. No one'd ever said that to me before. You see, I'd always said how proud I was to be fat, but it was really that I was proud to be famous and I'd often thought I should be much thinner. Not merely from the aesthetic point of view but for medical reasons, too. But Martha seemed to think otherwise. Then she said, could we have our photo taken together? I said, In the mirror? Because I couldn't see other-wise how it could be done. That's when I learnt no one had been taking those photos she'd been sending me, that she had a camera that was a remote control. You set it and there's about fifteen seconds to move back into the shot. She put it on a table and moved back into line and it gave a whirr and then click!

She explained how after she'd got my letter saying how the tour was off and I wouldn't be in Charleston, she'd been trying to call me for weeks and weeks and of course she didn't have my new phone number. She'd set off two days before when a friend'd given her a ride as far as New Orleans, where she'd stayed the night, and the next day she'd come on by the train through Houston. Some journey! Then when she got to Drake at last she'd felt too nervous to come straight up to see me, because of course she didn't even know if I'd be here. She still couldn't phone, so in the end she got the cab driver to bring up the message.

"A heck of a sight easier if I'd been in Charleston," I said.

"Oh, sure," she said. "Sure, but I understand, I do understand."

I tried to explain how I felt I was letting people down by pulling out but that I'd also have been letting people down by going ahead. I told her about the TV company and Hiram and how he'd kicked me. Martha said that probably Hiram was getting some kind of financial rake-off from the TV company and that was why he'd been so angry when I told him I was pulling out.

"You were dead right," she said. "Who needs that kind

212

of manager? A bloodsucker! I wish I could get my hands on him. I'd give him a kick with interest!"

The way she said that, in her deep voice: "A blood-sucker . . . !"

She went back to the Best Western, but in the evening she came see me again. She was wearing a kind of tight-fitting yellow satin dress, and she looked real good. Her skin was gleaming and her breasts looked like sausages ready to burst. She was carrying two bottles of tequila and some limes, and a knife she'd got with her to chop the limes, and we went in the kitchen and I watched as she chopped the limes and made margaritas. She was very practiced about it and she explained to me that she'd once worked in a bar in a hotel in Miami. That gave us more common ground in that we were able to share our experiences of hotel work. It was interesting, though tell the truth her hotel sounded more like a clip joint than a hotel, nothing like the Ranelagh Grand, which as I may've said makes its money from business conventions. Then I described my experience of being lifted bodily by the tornado and transported through the air, and I showed her the arm that was broken. I'd had problems with the arm because it hadn't set right the first time and had had to be rebroken, and the plaster wasn't that long off and the skin was still quite pink and tender, like the skin on a baby.

"It's perfect!" she said. "Bend it for me."

I tried. I couldn't bend it all the way, the elbow was too stiff. Though even before it was broken there was too much flesh on the arm to give a full bend.

213

She touched the elbow. "Is that where it's stiff?"

"Kind of." I could feel the touch of her fingers on the skin even after she'd stopped touching.

"Oh, but you were so unlucky!"

"No," I said, "I reckon I'm lucky. Because it made me understand how insignificant I am in the scale of things. I did a lot of thinking that night. I understood I was only ordinary."

She laughed. "You! Ordinary? Insignificant!" Then she looked down the hill. "It's such a beautiful spot here. So tranquil. I can't imagine people coming up here to see you."

"I've finished with that," I said. "I've quit."

"I know," she said. "I'm glad. I'm really glad."

"Are you?"

"Yeah, I am," she said. "Sometimes it's right to quit. If you feel it's right it's right, isn't it?" Then she drained her glass. "Where's that tequila?"

And we went back into the kitchen, where I put on some big steaks my ma'd left for me, and as we watched them cook we drank more and more tequila. She drank fast, even faster than me; we were on the second bottle inside of fifteen minutes.

I didn't ask why she was glad I'd called the show off, but I tried to explain my own reasoning, and I referred to the article Hilary showed me, about how I was running a freak show.

She laughed again. "What's a freak anyway? Aren't we all freaks? Who isn't a freak? It's a stupid word. Okay,

214

you're a freak, but the people who come to see you are freaks. I'm a freak too. Course I am. I'm a bigger freak than you."

"I don't buy that," I said. "You're only three hundred pound."

"Three hundred pounds of what? Three hundred pounds of neuroticism! Three hundred pounds of irrational thoughts and screwy desires and crazy fantasies and goddamn nightmares all jumbled up in together. My brain's a Pandora's box!"

I must have looked doubtful, because she puts down her glass, and says, "Look, Michael," and unbuttons the front of her dress. Underneath, she was wearing a black kind of slip, with shoulder straps. She slips one strap off.

The number of scars! Jesus, I couldn't believe it. Her body: the skin was covered with these thin, white lines, some long, some short, on her wrists, arms, legs, thighs, stomach, breasts, shoulders. Line after line after line, flanked by little dots, where the stitches went. I just couldn't believe how many there were.

She knew the dates of most of them. She'd say: yeah, that was ninety seventy-nine, the twentieth of August. That was nineteen eighty-two, the day before Thanksgiving. That was last year, the second of January, and, she said, "When I got one of your letters."

"You cut yourself on account of my letter?"

She shrugged. "It's partly as I hate myself when I do it. And partly that I love it. I love the way the flesh gets depressed under the blade; the pressure increases, and

215

suddenly the blade goes through and there's this warm feeling, the feeling of pain, which runs right through you. But I don't know why. I guess it's an urge. I've been to psychiatrists who say it's attention-seeking and self-loathing, but I don't reckon I am attention-seeking or self-loathing. I think it's more purgative." She paused. "What I have decided is not to fight it. Never fight it. When I get the urge, I give into it. Y'know? I go for it. I cut whenever I want. I just cut, I press the knife in and cut. D'you reckon I'm right?"

"Yeah," I say, but a little doubtfully.

"Do you?"

"Yeah. I guess so. If you need to—yeah. I mean, I guess it's your body, isn't it?"

She looks at me kind of breathless. "Where's that knife?"

"What knife?"

"The knife . . . I was doing the limes . . . anything. Have you got a razor?"

"Sure, I—"

Then she seizes a knife. Not the limes knife, as it happens—that was serrated, she later explained to me. Instead she got that buffalo burger knife I bought back in the Burgerland Experience, with the black horn handle. "Watch," she says. She holds out her arm, turning it to expose the soft fleshy underside, and presses the blade in, and it's just as she said, the flesh goes down and down and suddenly it seems to burst and the blade goes through and up comes the blood. She licks it.

216

"Here."

"What?"

"Go on. Go on."

I lick. There is a quantity of blood coming out. It tastes . . . sweet. But good.

"Go on," she says. "Here. Here."

Then I have an idea and get the tequila bottle and pour on a little. She gives a kind of shudder. I lick off the blood and the tequila, then I say, "Give me the knife," I say.

I take the bloody knife, I press it down, on my belly, on to one of the great rolls of fat which comprise my belly, and press slowly. Ever so slowly. The knife disappears, I don't even know if it's gone in as the flesh seems to fold over it like water, and I'm still pressing, still pressing and still licking her arm from which I can truly feel the pump of the heart from the blood coming out as I draw the blade slowly toward me, and the flesh expands and opens like a wide pink-white mouth and as the air hits it I feel the sting of pain and nothing seems to be happening but then the blood percolates out.

"Oh God, oh God, oh God," she says.

If you're fat you don't possess mobility, on a beanbag or anywhere else, at the best of times. You and the other person just sort of collide, you meet, you merge. And I was pretty drunk; she too. So I guess you could say that there was a lot of fumbling and stumbling over great tracts of unexplored flesh; so much flesh you could almost get lost. We were grappling away, our hands slipping and sliding. Her legs were these great slippery hams, I couldn't

217

get a grip at all, not that I can talk, mine are three times the size. We were both pretty drunk, like I say, and there was blood and tequila all over the place, and all the time the steaks were sizzling away in the pan. There was blue smoke everywhere, like there'd been some explosion. We were lucky there wasn't a fire, I guess.

Afterwards, I kiss my way round, along the scars which run, straight but not quite straight, from shoulder to breast, from breast to sternum, from sternum down to belly button, on and round and by and past and with and over. They keep on reminding me of something. What? What? At the time, I can't bring it to mind. Only later that night, as we lie together in the darkness, which seems quite kind and soft as velvet, with the house making its familiar little sounds, and I reach out and feel the smooth convex drum of her belly, and the little soft bumpy ridges of the scars—I get it. Don't laugh: the tracks of the pioneer railroads built all over America in the nineteenth century. You know?

Like a map.

The morning was bright and fine, but we didn't see too much of it. I woke first and I couldn't decide whether to wake her or not. I got up and let Lincoln out, and heated up some grits and donuts. She was still sleeping, and seeing as how she was going to have to head off to Fort Worth I thought I'd better wake her up, but first I put on some music. I wanted to put on something she'd like to wake to, so I put on the first side of *Will the Circle be Unbroken?* by the Nitty-Gritty Dirt Band, which I reckon is possibly my favorite album of all time. Before waking her up I waited till the second track, "Keep on the Sunny Side," which is a lovely gentle song. It's a beautiful song. I've got it on tape as well and I often used to play it to myself when I was sitting in the Shrine, over and over again. "Keep on the sunny side, always on the sunny side, keep on the sunny side of life . . ." Not like that, I can't sing at all. It's sung by Mother Maybelle Carter. Anyway when she started to sing I woke up Martha, and she stretched like a cat.

"Hey," she says, "it's the 'Sunny Side'! What time is it?"

"About noon," I say. "What time's your train?"

"Oh," she says, looking kind of shocked, "I'm not sure about that. I'm not sure."

I told her about the times of the various trains. I knew those, they hadn't changed for years. What I really wanted to find out was how long she was planning on staying in Fort Worth and if after that she might be coming back this way. She listened, and then she rolled on one side and stood up. "Michael," she says, in her husky voice, "I may not actually go to Fort Worth at all."

After all that tequila the night before and everything, I was a little dazed. I couldn't see what she meant. I said, "But this friend in Fort Worth . . . if you want to call him up . . ."

"Oh, forget about him," she says. "He doesn't exist, I made him up. I was never going to Fort Worth, why'd I want to go to Fort Worth?" And she looks at me in a kind of lazy way, and picks up the burger knife and traces her finger down the blade, very lightly. "I came to see you, Michael. That's why I came. I wanted to see you."

A day or so later, while Martha was still in Drake, still staying at the Best Western, I was dozing on the beanbags and thinking about the rich and famous and everyone else, and how it's like one of the parties you get in one of those big oil mansions down round Austin or Houston. Helicopter pad, great sweeps of floodlit lawn, white marquees, lackeys with trays of pink champagne. Warm, evening air. There's maybe a hundred, two hundred guests, the men in tuxedos, and up on a stage, along with a pianist and guy playing the sax, a lady in pearls and a long slinky low-cut black dress with a wasp waist is singing something quite slow and melodious . . . But, just outside the floodlit area, in the darkness, all the way round, are tangled rolls of razor wire, and beyond the wire is everyone else. Crowds and crowds and crowds pressing in, stretching away. They're looking in at the party and hearing the clink of glasses and the laughter and the singing, and recognizing a few familiar faces. Look, there's Elvis Presley talking to Buddy Holly and . . . and, see, there's Grace Kelly and Marilyn Monroe and Bob Hope, and Jack Kennedy and Aretha Franklin and Johnny Cash and Jim Reeves. Everyone in the crowd's hoping they might join that party and get a slice of the action, people are so desperate they're even fixed on trying to cut through the razor wire but this is funny razor wire, magic wire, it joins itself back the moment you cut it.

Some do, of course. Bust in on the party. By mysterious, undivulged means. The wire parts like magic, like the Red

Sea for Moses in the Bible, and they're stepping through, and you see them claim their glasses of champagne off the waiters.

Then there're other people who think they've got in, but the wire closes and they get caught.

That's me. Truth is, I never really bust in. I thought I'd got the wire cut but it always mended itself before I was through. I was nearly famous. Mickey, the nearly famous fat man, that's me. The Colossus of Drake, a nearly city in the South of the United States of America. Hi. Glad to meet you. How ya doing? Wanna guess my weight? Six hundred, seven hundred. Keep going . . .

When Martha came up to see me—she spent most the time up with me, although she kept on her room at the Best Western—I tried describing some of this to her. She listened very carefully, very thoughtfully. That's one thing I'd say about Martha, she's a very thoughtful woman, she's a good listener. What she said was this, she said: "Sure, Michael, but if you think of it from their point of view, the people inside the wire . . . to them it's like they're in the penitentiary. They can't get out! The wire that keeps you out also keeps them in."

I say, "What about the helicopter pad?"

"Forget the helicopter pad," she says. "They've got the wire round their brains. But that's not the big thing," she says, "the big thing is, if you look round, in the darkness, if you turn round so you're not dazzled by the lights and you let your eyes adjust to the darkness, aren't there plenty other parties going on?"

221

"Are there?"

"Sure there are," she says. "Sure. You don't have to press up against the barbed wire, you don't have to try cutting your way through. You don't need to. None of us need to. You just go on and join another party, or start up your own. Okay, it's not floodlit, and it may not have the stars and the glitter, but it can still be a real good party."

I guess she's right. (Though I'm always saying that, she says; I'm always saying: "I guess you're right." And I say, hearing her, "I guess you're right.") But I guess she is right, I mean about everything. If you don't like a party, go to another. If you don't like your life, start up a new one. That's the American way.

Thinking about that, in those days after she'd gone back home, I found myself considering how, if Martha and me got married, we might have a real party. Everybody could come, all the family, Ma and Zoe and her boyfriend the mountaineer, and Hilary and her dinosaur husband and their two kids, and Uncle Vince, and even Uncle Bobby and Anya. Just imagine it. The whole family, together, for the first time since Pa's funeral. And I thought I could invite along other people I knew, like . . . well, I don't know. But there'd be Martha's folks, too. She's got three brothers and two sisters, all younger than her.

I knew I didn't want to be married here. I wanted someplace with romance, like tying the knot on a steam train going through the Rockies. That's what some folk do. You can hire an entire train. But, logistically, given my weight, that's maybe not practicable, and there's the cost to consider. So I reckoned the best place in town had to be the Ranelagh Grand. We'd have ourselves photographed in front of the fountain, in front of the Grecian goddess with the waters coming out of the flowers. She'd have Texas yellow roses in her hair, Martha would, and I'd be wearing a black tuxedo jacket, white tuxedo shirt, and black string tie. That was my idea.

I didn't put it to Martha for a long, long while. Not for months and months. She went back to Dorchester, and then visited me again, twice. In the end, however, I put to her the notion. What I'm trying to say is: I proposed marriage. Don't laugh. Proposing marriage—Jee-sus, what a nerve! Who'd want to marry the Colossus of Drake? Not an appealing prospect, you wouldn't have thought. Not a major turn-on. Considering a handsome intelligent woman like Martha, I didn't reckon I had a prayer. And I was real nervous. Was I nervous! I was sick with nerves. I had flutterings in my belly like I had a swarm of fruit bats in there! However, she just nodded and smiled: "That's fine by me, Michael. I'd love that. I thought you'd never ask."

Then we fell to discussing the menu.

7

I'm a private person right now. I've done these tapes for you mainly as a matter of setting the historical record straight, because there are some funny things've been written in the newspapers, as I've said. It's taken me about a month, all in all. I never thought I'd have so much to say, at the start. I hope it's what you want, and I'd like to say here I'm sorry if I've repeated myself and not told the story as straight as I'd meant to; it's hard knowing what's relevant. But also I'd like to thank you for asking me to take part in the project. I've enjoyed doing it, getting things ordered in my mind, working it all out, it's been more interesting than I ever thought it'd be. It gets your life into a perspective. Most of the time, I don't know why, but after I've finished a recording, I've found myself thinking of my pa. I owe him a lot, I should've said. He was just forty-six when he passed on. I knew he was sick but I didn't know how sick, no one'd told me. Maybe he didn't want any fuss made, or maybe it was Ma who decided not to tell me how sick he was. When he passed on, it was one of those kind of nothing days, gray and dull and nothing. It was in the fall. Chuck Watson gave me the message down at the Ranelagh Grand that I was to call home, he says do it from his office and that's what I did and how I found out how he'd passed on, in the hospital. He had cancer of the lung. I guess that's why I don't like folk smoking tobacco, on account of that. Mr. Watson gave me time off. "Take a week, Michael," he said. "You come back when you're ready. Take all the time you need." That was good of him, some employers would've acted different to that. He probably understood because it occurred not long after his son was killed, in a Jet Ski accident, up on Lake Constant. I don't know what happened exactly, he never talked about it but, someone told me he must've hit a floating log. It's a danger for Jet Skiers. What happens is this: you get a dead tree falling in the water and it gets waterlogged and sinks to the bottom, but then it lightens and rises up and hangs just below the surface. It was a big tragedy for Mr. Watson, losing his son. He was his only son. I remember seeing him afterwards, Mr. Watson, after the funeral, and he looked all crumpled up, it was like the air'd been sucked out of him. So probably all that was sitting in his mind when he told me to take off all the time I wanted.

I went straight to the depot and caught the first train out for Constant. I often think about that train journey. Nothing happened on it. I looked out and saw the country bumping past, the little houses on the outskirts of Drake and trees and scattered farmsteads and horses, and one horse I recall must've been scared by the train and it ran away with its back hooves kicking up, and suddenly I felt real scared too, I felt how fragile it all was, I felt the world was about to come to an end any moment, and everyone else'd be catapulted up out of their seats in the direction of Heaven and I'd be left on the train by myself, and even if I managed to slow that train down and jump off at Constant I wouldn't find no one there except maybe all the bad people that'd been left behind. I was quite upset, I was very upset. I kept thinking of Pa in his workshop sawing away, and the smell of the wood and the rasp of the plane and the sight of the sawdust he used to get in his hair, and I just wished I could've said good-bye to him, I wished I could've thanked him. It's corny stuff, but that's how it is. Everything's easy in hindsight. He was buried in Rough Creek Cemetery like I told you, and when Uncle Bobby let the coffin slip off of his shoulder and it dropped in the grave, for weeks and weeks I kept hearing the crack when it hit the ground, it gave me nightmares. Even now it sends a chill through me, I get goose bumps at the thought of it. And afterward when I came back to Drake I kind of felt I'd lost my way, like the trail had given out and left me alone in the wilderness, and it's curious but one thing I've learnt from doing these tapes, is that it was after all that happened and my pa passed on that I began to put on the weight.

So, what is there to conclude? I don't know. But something occurs to me, I should've asked this before: what's going to happen to these tapes? I think what happened with President Richard Nixon, all those private tapes he made in the White House suddenly becoming public property, and it occurs to me I should maybe listen through to all this, just to check it over. I don't want to cause any offense to anyone. I don't want this put out over the radio. I mean, I'm private, as I say. I've changed my telephone number. I do still get fan mail, though less than I used to, and I reply as best I can, and occasional requests from newspapers and TV. Canadian . . . a Canadian TV company the other day. I said no without too much trouble, without even waiting to hear how much they were willing to pay. Of course I wondered afterwards. Five hundred dollars? Five thousand dollars? Another company, a Japanese company, wants to do a full movie. I don't know how they heard about us, somebody must've told them, but I'm not doing it. They say it's a great story, I say there's no story at all. There's no story, the only story is we're fat. That's the only interest. Something to laugh at, ha ha, hee hee. Something to prod, to poke. See these elasticized nylon briefs—wanna try them on for size? Then the casual question slipped in by the interviewer as an afterthought, while the camera zooms in close up: oh, and excuse me, but could you give us some idea how a couple fat as you two ever gets together in bed, is it possible? Well, forget it. I'm not interested, Martha's not interested either. There'd be people everywhere, fixing up lights, taping cables . . . it'd be the same experience over again. Anyway, I'm not in favor of . . . I mean the Japanese. I'm not prejudiced, but the entire U.S. national economy is under threat from cheap Japanese goods.

The way I see it, Martha and me, we're what the journalists call a non-story. We're ordinary people, or ordinary enough. Ordinary inasmuch as anyone's ordinary, which they aren't. That's what people don't understand. Like I say, our brains are the same size as everybody else's. If I died and someone took my brain into a laboratory, they wouldn't be able to tell it was anything out of the ordinary, it was the brain of a fat man. Would they? You tell me, I'm no biologist. Would they be able to tell? Any more than they could tell I was an American?

I'm not saying I'll never do another interview. Money might become a consideration. But Martha's got some, and I've got some more put by, the proceeds of the business, though Hiram seems to've gotten away with most of it. There's enough for a couple of years, put it like that, then we'll see. I'm only twenty-six. The future's wide open. I do know I want to stay in Drake, I know that, and I know that if I was talented enough, I'd like to do something like Pa did, and make something beautiful, like that chair with the armadillo. But I know my limitations. I couldn't never do anything like that. First thing I've got lined up is my business manual. I've let that slip a little but I feel kind of mentally tuned up for it now. I've got a working title for it, "The Fat Man's Guide to Business." Not quite snappy enough, but it'll do for the moment. It's going to be a distillation of my personal experiences seen from the business perspective, with advice and information for the novice entrepreneur. When the book's finished my plan is to have it published by one of the big publishing companies in Houston. Or New York, maybe. Just so long as the marketing's good. I want it distributed all over the States, I want it in every bookstore, every airport.

Some hope. Dream on, daddy-o. Still, you never know. It may open a few doors, but even if it doesn't there're plenty of possibilities. I'm considering my options, put it like that. What I'm thinking is, after the wedding, I may get into real estate. You see Drake's expanding, there's a building boom, and Martha's pa's a construction engineer. And sometimes I think . . . sometimes I think I wouldn't even mind building a big hotel, with fountains and marble floors like the Ranelagh Grand, and a beautiful big pool. Which I, being the owner, could use as and when I desired! But don't worry, I'm not going to turn into another wizened old Leonard Saker, grumbling about the service, and doing spot-checks, and looking for traces of dust to catch out the staff. No, I'd run it along more friendly, personal lines.

We're holding the wedding in the Ranelagh Grand. Where else? It's in two months' time. When I said to Martha, how about the Ranelagh Grand, she was a little doubtful. She said, "Michael, I'm not against it, it's just I've a certain history of not agreeing too well with revolving doors," but I told her that wasn't a problem, we could get in the back way through the kitchens. Mr. Tiplady's still there, he'll just have to put up with it for once and let us through. But everyone's coming. We haven't issued the invitations yet, but everyone's coming. After the celebratory dinner, after night's fallen, we're all going to have a swim in the hotel pool. All the guests, by order, Michael. No it's not compulsory, but I guess every-one'll join in. I can imagine it already: the lights being turned out one by one, like at the theater, till we can barely see each other and we're just floating in the dark. Though I know it's unbiblical I'd say at a guess that's maybe what Heaven's like, voices and sounds, the swish of warm water and the occasional mystery collision of flesh.

So I'll wind it up now. I've plenty to do before the wedding. Martha's away in Dorchester right now, but she's coming back tomorrow, and Zoe's coming too, and the day after that I'm being measured for my wedding suit.

Me and Martha. It's such a joy. We talk a lot, when she's here. It's good talking. We talk about all kind of things, not just the wedding, but food and sleeping, and crime (we're both big on crime), and the present condition of the United States of America. Many of our views, both political and ethical, seem to coincide. Like me, she happens to believe the United States has a duty to the rest of the world to remain world leader, and that we must not start cozying up to the Soviets; like me, she is concerned about Cuba and Mexico. Politicians in Washington have woken up to Nicaragua, but they don't see what's happening in Mexico. It's always the same, destabilization of the economy leads to political destabilization, and that's when the Reds see their opportunity to foment revolution.

We also talk about our feelings and emotions. It's therapeutic talking about emotions, Martha says.

Then we cut each other a lot, usually using something like a steak knife. Not razors, they go in too quick. The pressure's what's so exciting. The slow, steady pressure and knowing the flesh is going to give, then the give, and the taste of the blood. Sometimes we cut each other, sometimes we cut ourselves simultaneously. Never our faces. Legs, thighs, arms, bellies . . . I know, I know, I know . . . you must think I'm crazy. Self-mutilation! Jesus! It's not wholesome, it's sick! Only unhappy people cut themselves! I know. That's the received opinion. That's why I haven't told Ma, or anyone much. Certainly not Hilary. I mean if Hilary ever finds out I know what she'll say, she'll say we both need urgent psychiatric help.

Well, all I can say is, sure; but maybe you'd feel different if you were saddled with a body like mine. Because, and here I'm speaking for myself, not for Martha, when I cut myself I always feel strangely lighter. It's like there's a release from the body, like something that's been trapped in the body is escaping through the cut in the skin. Like a gas, or something. Or like me, escaping, leaving my body behind, that's nearer it. Tell the truth, for a few moments, just when the cut's been made, it no longer feels like my body at all, it's just a heavy, soft, flabby cushion of a thing to which I happen to be connected. The freedom! It's a wonderful sensation. Okay, maybe I won't go on doing it for ever, maybe it's just a temporary thing, maybe one day I'll pick up the knife and think no, that's not for me, I've had enough of that, I don't know, but just at the moment I don't see any particularly good reason why I ought to be apologetic or ashamed about it. There's nothing in the Bible to say you should or shouldn't cut yourself, it's not a sin. And it's not against the Constitution. So what's it matter? Whose body is it? This is the United States, a free country, the freest of countries, and it hurts no one. Martha and I tape ourselves up when we've finished, and it's kind of miraculous how quick the body heals itself up. Just leaving behind these little scars. I'm getting quite a network of them, as a record of our lovemaking.

I told Martha about these tapes, by the way, and the oral history project, and she reckons it's an interesting idea, getting recordings of lots of people in the area, building up a picture of the whole community. Each one like a piece of the jigsaw. She said how great it would be to have tapes of all those who sailed on the *Mayflower*! I pointed out, the tape recorder hadn't been invented! But you know what she means. I mean I'm no one much but in fifty years, a hundred years, when America has set up its first colonies on Mars, just like the Pilgrim Fathers, folk'll be able to listen to these tapes and say, hey, what d'ya know, there was once this fat guy, this truly fat, fat guy, the fattest guy who's ever lived in Drake, and this is his voice! Reedy, squeaky . . . And I'll be speaking to them, telling my life story, to this point in the early fall of nineteen eighty-four, *anno Domini*, the year of our Lord Jesus Christ. I keep saying I've given up on fame but still it's a pleasant thought that maybe through these tapes I'll achieve a kind of fame after all, even a kind of immortality, even if I may not be present in bodily form to take account of it. I'll be watching from Heaven, though. I'll be watching from Heaven. Keeping my ears cocked. Holding the old steak knife.

I don't know what they'll think of me, back on Earth. I'd like to know. Something like: sure he may have had

232

his ups and downs, but he never gave up. He kept on trying. Something like that. And that he was the nearly heaviest man in all America, and that thanks to Providence he met the most beautiful girl in the world. Like a fairy tale. I know, it's corny stuff. It's enough to make your flesh squirm. If you saw it in a movie you probably wouldn't believe it, you'd probably walk out. But it's beautiful too. That's how I think.

When she's not here, like now, I sometimes feel I'm like that mangy old crock of a man I told you about who lived in the old chicken shack before I was here, sitting and staring into space with his gun on his knees, hoping to shoot a ghost. Not that I'm doing that. I'm just waiting for Martha to call. What else do I do? Well, I'm doing these tapes. In addition, well . . . I don't know. I don't know. Scratch around. Wash, cook, do the dishes, watch TV, listen to Teddy Montezuma on the "Country Hour", call up some donuts. Talk with Lincoln. Okay he doesn't talk back, but he brings me the occasional mouse. A rat not long ago, half alive, bleeding. Dumped it on the floor, tail twitching (that's Lincoln's tail, not the rat's).

What else? There's reading, I try reading. The *Constant Bulletin*, the *Drake Chronicle*, the Bible. Sometimes a *Reader's Digest*. I fall asleep, generally. The other day I tried reading John Steinbeck's *Mice and Men* and I fell asleep almost soon as I put my hands on it and opened a page, and I can't recall a thing it was about, except it seemed quite sad. Sleep does come over me a lot, real deep sleep, black sleep. It's the flesh, pulling me down, dragging me under, I guess. Half of the United States population seems to be on sleeping pills these days, but I just reach for a book and my eyes are shutting like the two of them was linked by some force.

I prefer thinking to reading. I spend a lot of time doing that. Ma says it's a dangerous business thinking too much, but I like it. Recently I was thinking about fat and diabetic . . . it's not a recipe for a long life. I know that, sure, I know. I could drop dead at any time. My kidneys could pack it in, I could have a stroke. But I'd like to say two or three things in response to that. First, following Dr. Coughlan's advice, I have recently made certain changes in my diet. Less fatty foods, more carbohydrates and fruits and vegetables. And lately I have formed the impression, no more than an impression, based on nothing concrete, that I may be a little lighter than I was. I could currently be no more than seven hundred pound, or less. Am I kidding myself? Possibly, but if I put my hand on my belly I feel some kind of shrinkage may be taking place. It's kind of surprising. Where will it end? Where's the river flowing? Trouble is, I'm not sure I'd want to lose too much weight. I like fat, Martha likes fat. I wouldn't like being thin, scraggy. I'm not giving up on all my favorite foods, I've told Dr. Coughlan that and I reckon he understands my views on the matter. You see, I'm not afraid of a short life. I mean it's the same for all of us, fat and thin when you come to think of it, death's with us all, it's got its claws in our brains, only we pretend it hasn't. I see my body and realize it's as much like death as life. And what I reckon is what matters isn't

234

how long your stay is on earth, it's how much life you pack into that stay. One man can pack more into thirty years than another gets into seventy. I'm thinking for instance of President Jack Kennedy. Each day's a blessing. A privilege. The sun shines, the sky's blue, the birds are singing. To be alive, to be in love, to be American—who's grumbling? Not me. Not Michael.

Well, here's another surprise for you: I've taken up traveling. The King of Fat, the Colossus of Drake—he travels. Well, in my mind. Sure. Fantasy travel. I'm still here on my beanbags, but I move about to all kind of places. I stroll down to the old C-J Works and pick up my staple gun, or I'm at Jackson's having a few warm sugary donuts or honey waffles and a strawberry milk shake before moseying on to the burger bar or the pizzeria and then on to the Ranelagh Grand where I wear my green and gold uniform and carry the bags over to the elevators, and I feel free and happy and light. That's the oddest damn feeling, feeling light. Gravity's had its hold on me for so long now, sucking me earthward, and now I'm suddenly free of it, or not free but one-sixth free, like those moon astronauts, bouncing along, doing their moon dance. One of them, I recall, sang that song, you know? Instead of singing, "I was strolling in the park one day," he sang; "I was strolling on the moon one day . . . " It may have been Eugene Cernan, on Apollo Seventeen was it. He lives in Houston, I'm told, he's a businessman. Alan Bean lives in Houston too. He was the third or the fourth to step on the moon on Apollo Twelve and he's now an artist.

Someone told me, he does these big oil paintings of the moon and space. What I also recall being told, he's got these little dogs living in his home and ya-ya-yapping all the time and when he wants some silence he fires at them with a water pistol. Psssh! One quick squirt! Then they're quiet. Psssh! Even the sight of the raised water pistol stops their yapping.

These are truly famous men, and I can't really begin to imagine what their lives must be like after visiting the moon, but I can imagine the sensation of walking on the moon. Bouncing along, doing the moon dance. Bounce, bounce, bounce! Whoa! Take it easy, take it easy . . . It's a great sensation, like not being fat at all. I don't know I can describe it to exactitude. You recall what I told you how at the last trumpet the dead are going to burst out of their graves and float up to heaven. Think of it: Martha and me, hand in hand, flying upwards, in the greatest tornado of them all. Not an F-four or an F-five but an F-ten! No I don't believe it's going to happen quite like that, I'm not that dumb, as Hiram'd say, but sometimes when we cut ourselves I get a sensation of what it might be like, that last flight in the darkness toward the stars: the rush of air, the effortlessness, the exhilaration, the lights of the earth fading beneath us. Especially when we cut ourselves, pressing down nice and slow, till the flesh gives way and the blood wells up.

Martha's coming back tomorrow, and she'll meet Zoe. For the first time. I'm looking forward to that. I guess that's why I'm in such a good mood. Sir Isaac got it wrong, gravity don't exist. Weight don't exist. No sir!

Zoe, she's my younger sister. Have I told you about her? I can't recall now exactly what I may've told you. She's twenty-four, with short shiny black hair that curls up below her chin, and kind of gleams in the sun. Her teeth do, too. She has lovely white teeth, perfect teeth, like a movie star. She's a lovely person. She's not at all like Hilary. I don't mean that as a criticism, just Hilary's always very serious and high-minded, whereas Zoe's funny. She looks on the funny side. She's got a boyfriend in Tyler who's a mountaineer. True! Not that there're any mountains round Tyler. He must find the mountains someplace else. That's what he does, he climbs mountains. And someone pays him, I guess, for the privilege.

I haven't met him yet, but Zoe comes to see me every fortnight to drive me to Dr. Coughlan's. Drives up in the truck, hooting hullo. Her horn's three-toned: low, middle, high. Last time, after I'd had my tests at the clinic, we stocked up at the G. T. Robbins grocery store. We loaded up the truck with bread, meat, pasta, cakes, rice, vanilla pudding, ice cream, beer, tequila, all the rest of everything. And we'd driven home, and were unloading—not that I'm much help, still I give a kind of moral support—when I ask her something that's been bugging me all along. "Zoe," I say, "Zoe, do you recall that visit we had to the Blue Falls? And us throwing in the branch?"

"With Pa?"

"Yeah, not with Ma, she stayed at home. But everyone else."

She frowns—though with Zoe it's not really a frown,

her forehead stays quite clear. It's more like a mental frown. "I recall the falls. I even recall us all getting in the pickup, before we started out. Then we had to get out again."

"Because we were too heavy."

"No," she says, "because you wanted to go to the john."

"I don't recall that," I say. "Me?"

"And we had to sit and wait for near on half an hour."

"I don't recall that at all. Sure it was me?"

"I can see it now," she says, "We were going crazy, waiting for you."

"I thought the reason was we were so heavy the undercarriage was scraping."

"No, you had to go to the john," she said. "You were ages. You were always doing that. Just when we were about to go off somewhere you always did it. Maybe not half an hour, but it felt like it."

I didn't agree, I don't think I ever did that. However, she seemed convinced. Anyway she went on unpacking but I wanted to get this sorted out, so I said to her, "But d'you recall the big branch we threw in?"

"When we were at the falls? No."

"It was the morning after camping. Pa was fishing, and we walked back above the falls and threw it in together. A big branch."

Zoe pauses holding a box of food in her arms. "Michael," she says, "which trip was this you're talking about?"

"Well," I say, "there was only ever one trip to the Blue Falls. And this was the one."

"Okay, but I don't recall the branch. I recall us crossing the railroad. I recall how hot it was. I recall Uncle Bobby's blister."

"But Uncle Bobby wasn't there!"

"Sure he was," she says. "Uncle Bobby? Sure!"

"But he wasn't," I say. "I mean I know it was his pickup, but Pa was driving."

"Michael he was there," she insists. "He was!" And, seeing the look of doubt on my face: "I could even tell you what he was wearing. He had a Stetson on his head. He was real worried about snakes. And he got a blister on his toe."

And, now she mentioned it, I did recall the blister. We were climbing the bluff and Uncle Bobby took off his shoe and showed us the blister, on the end of his big toe. His toe was big and yellow and on the end was this tiny red blip of a blister sitting on the end. Everyone laughed, he was really grumpy. Yeah, I recalled that well enough.

"And what a fuss he made!" says Zoe. "Like it was a mortal wound, the way he carried on!"

I said how we ought to ask Hilary if she remembered Uncle Bobby's blister, if she wasn't too busy singing with her glee club. "Her glee club—what is it about glee clubs?" Zoe says. "What is it they sing?" So I told her: "They sing 'Chattanooga Choo Choo'."

"Are you kidding? 'Chattanooga Choo Choo'? Hilary?" She laughs, we both laugh.

"No, but do you recall—" I begin, just as she does the same. "No," I say, "you go ahead."

"You go ahead, Michael," she says. "I wasn't going to say anything."

"No, nor was I."

There's a pause then. Then she says: "No, I was just thinking, d'you recall us carving our names on the rock?"

At that I was suddenly excited, it was like something came to life in my head. I forgot all about the branch I'd been wanting to ask her about. "What's this rock? What's this rock? What rock?"

"There was this shiny black rock we carved our names on. Not where we camped, not down by the gorge. Further up, right by the falls. We all carved our names."

I stared at her. It was really exciting. The whole moment swam back to me, like in a picture, this big glistening gleaming slab of rock, very smooth, like a tablet out of the Bible, and how in the morning after striking camp we knelt by it one by one and scratched our names on it with one of the tent pegs. I could recall the moment, how the rock was wet, because it was just below the lip of the falls and spray was drifting through the air, and how after Hilary handed me the peg I knelt down—I could kneel then—and the morning sun was shining through the spray, making these beautiful rainbows. It was like praying, kneeling there among the rainbows, with the deafening roar of the falls in your ears. Hilary had already carved her name, and above her name was Pa's, and he'd carved his name very beautifully, as you'd expect, with kind of almost Gothic-type lettering, and I wanted to carve my name like his, and I took a long time. I don't know how

240

long, but a long time. Zoe was next in line and she kept on telling me to hurry up and give her the peg, but I didn't want to hurry, and in the end she got bored and walked off. When I finally finished my name I looked up, and I nearly died, my heart stopped, because there she was, near the edge of the falls, cartwheeling. Cartwheeling among the rainbows. I wasn't scared. I ought've been scared she was going to cartwheel right over the edge, because the edge was quite crumbly, you could tell bits had broken off in the past, but I wasn't. I somehow knew she'd be all right, and she was, she was. My little sister, doing cartwheel after cartwheel.

I'm still staring at her. "D'you recall the rainbows in the spray? And cartwheeling?"

"Sure," she says. "Well I was always cartwheeling. I recall the rainbows. Weren't they beautiful?"

Once we've unloaded the groceries I open up some bags of potato chips, hickory-cured bacon chips, which is my favorite, and two cans of beer. Then we sit in the backyard, drinking beer and eating the chips, looking over the picket fence between the young palms. The sun's out, and Zoe's hair's shining, it's glossy. Everything feels real quiet and peaceful. The town's kind of humming beneath us, the traffic, but real soft, like a murmur of bees, and there's a dog you can hear somewhere barking way off but nothing else. I can see Lincoln in the long grass, hunting, the tip of his tail twitching like he hopes he's about to catch something.

"Y'know," says Zoe after a time; but she doesn't go on.

"What?" I ask.

241

"Nothing," she says. "It's just I was thinking, they're probably still there."

"Who?"

"The names. The names we carved on that rock below the falls. We could go back and look at them sometime."

"I don't know I could make it," I say. "You could. I couldn't make it."

"Sure you could," she says lazily. "Somehow. I don't know how. Me and Martha can get you there. We can lower you by helicopter."

For half a second I kind of thought maybe she was right, maybe I could get there somehow. Not by helicopter, but in a truck or something. Though a truck'd never be able to get up the bluff, it's far too steep. But maybe, just maybe, I thought, if I went on shedding weight, if I could shed more and more weight, I could struggle there on foot, with God's help. And then, once that half second passed, I knew I was kidding myself. I'd never get to the Blue Falls again. Never ever. There was no real trail or anything, after the railroad. Besides, Pa wouldn't be there, so what would be the point?

I didn't mind too much. I felt too lazy to mind, in the sunshine. All the memories of that trip were flooding through my mind, and how I was going on ten, and not that fat, and Pa was still alive. And everything was new and perfect. I thought of camping, and lighting the fire, and the faces flickering in the firelight, and falling asleep to the never-ceasing roar of the water, and that branch, sticking up like the antlers of a stag, moving toward the lip, not knowing what was about to happen, and how it hung on the lip before tipping forward into nothingness. And that rock. And Zoe, cartwheeling among the rainbows . . . But it wasn't like the memories were separate, detached; they were joined together like a single electric vision in three hundred and sixty degree, like a vision of Heaven, and as it reached me I felt just like I might've felt when I was there. Not exactly happy, happy's not the word, it doesn't quite cover the feeling adequately. More like contented, and light, beautifully light. Just floating away, like thistledown. And I realized, then and there, that I could get to the Blue Falls anytime I wanted. I didn't have to go physically, in person, I didn't need to go there in person. I could travel in my head.

I finish my beer, and lie back, staring at the blue sky. It's so blue, so blue. Then I roll on my side and look at Zoe. "Zoe," I say, "d'you recall Pa saying how the falls would go on and on to the end of time, till they were switch off by God?"

Zoe thinks for a while. "No," she says, with a smile. "No, I don't recall that. I don't recall that at all."

★

I can't think of much more to add right now. It's late, and I'm dead tired, and we're near the end of the tape. Can't be more than a couple of minutes left. So I'm going to hit the sack. Martha and Zoe are coming tomorrow, I want to be good and fresh. Want to freshen up the house, too. Shift the dust. Get some air moving through the place. Twelve hours' time, they'll be here.

It's a beautiful night out there. Drake's below, all lit up. There's a quantity of new building in progress and I can see a huge illuminated crane on the far side of the town, and the dark of the hills. A gentle, warm, friendly breeze's blowing up out of Mexico. Beyond the hills, there're the stars all scattered, like one of those settlements out in frontier country. The Dog Star, the Pole Star, what is it about stars? Mostly nothing, I guess. Still, I wouldn't like not to have them there.

On the subject of stars, incidentally, if you ever happen to come to Drake and need someplace to stay for the night, I'd like to make a recommendation of the Best Western. It's only two-star, and the Adelaide's three and the Ranelagh Grand's still four, but the Best Western's value for money. And it's pretty clean and decent. There's no swimming pool, but the coffee shop's good and the cheesecake's perfect. Very creamy, and not too thick a base. Chuck Watson's the manager now, since he moved over from the Ranelagh Grand. He's a good man . . . you could mention my name to him. Either Michael or Mickey, doesn't matter. Or just say the King of Fat. The Colossus of Drake. He'll know. Might even give you a discount. Sure, I'd take the Best Western if I were you, particularly if you have a liking for cheesecake.

I've nothing more to say. Except I don't rightly know why I told that last story. That story about Zoe and me talking about the Blue Falls and Zoe cartwheeling in the rainbows. Tell the truth, I'd cut it out if I were you. Cut it out with a razor. It doesn't signify. It's just a story. It doesn't signify anything at all.

AN INTERVIEW WITH
CHRISTOPHER NICHOLSON

The following Q& A touches on some of the author's thoughts and inspirations for the book. For a fuller exploration of these topics and ideas, please go to www.constablerobinson.com.

It may surprise some readers to learn that you're English. How did you come to write a novel like *The Fattest Man in America*?

During the late 1980s I visited America's Bible Belt to make a radio programme about the idea of the Apocalypse. There I met Christians who believed that the world was soon to come to a sudden end, with an event known as the Rapture. Those who had been born again would be swept up to heaven in an instant, while everyone else would be left behind. What intrigued me was the ease with which this radical belief seemed to sit inside a brash business culture. I didn't have any thought that it might be one of the ingredients to stir into a novel, but I tucked it away in my mind.

Did the process of making radio programmes help in creating a credible American voice for Mickey?

Yes, it did. If you make lots of radio programmes you soon become very attuned to voices and speech patterns. I quickly picked up on the distinctiveness of Texan speech. I have always been fascinated by the differences between the way people speak and the way they write. One of the challenges of fiction, I think, is to communicate the fluidity of the spoken word.

Is Mickey based on a particular individual?

Among the starting points for the novel was a remarkable photograph that I chanced to see on the front of an issue of *Granta* magazine in 1992. It showed a phenomenally fat man – so fat that his body no longer seemed quite credible – lying in a dark room. Much later, long after writing the novel, I learnt that the man was an American who had fought in the Korean War. His experiences left him with post-traumatic stress disorder and, bizarre as it seems, he decided to eat himself to death. The photograph was taken when he was exhibiting himself in a freak show that toured the States. I think that if I'd known this man's history I might have found the novel more difficult to write. Mickey is an entirely fictional character – although there really are people in the States as fat as him.

What were the literary influences on you as you wrote the novel?

I didn't have any writers looking over my shoulder. In hindsight, I'm aware that the story owes something to a minor, and largely defunct, tradition of Christian writing in which repentant sinners confess their evil deeds and describe how they found God. I should also say that I am an admirer of Daniel Defoe's novels, especially of *Moll Flanders* and *Robinson Crusoe*, and it has sometimes interested me to think of Mickey as a sort of Crusoe, in the sense that he is shipwrecked, marooned.

At one point in the novel, Mickey approvingly describes the United States as a fat country. Should one see your novel as a critique of American culture?

'A critique' implies a rather cool, analytical look, and I'm not sure that fits with how I think of the novel. I obviously wrote it out of a preoccupation with American culture, or at least with the larger-than-life version of American culture that you can find in Texas. It's all but impossible to ignore the United States nowadays; the country is part of everyone's cultural agenda, like it or not. In one regard at least, however, Mickey is quite un-American. The stereotypical American hero is a man of action, whereas most of the action in Mickey's life takes place inside his head.

The novel is very interested in the conflict between Mickey's material circumstances and his spiritual self. How does this dialogue between flesh and spirit reflect your own views?

I don't think of the opposition of flesh and spirit in a narrow religious sense. But I do remember, at school, the electric moment when I came across Wordsworth's lines: 'The world is too much with us; late and soon, getting and spending, we lay waste our powers'. I felt then, and still feel, that Wordsworth was right. Obviously there has to be a certain amount of getting and spending, but we live in a very materialistic age, and it's easy for people to be corrupted by materialism and to lose touch with their spiritual selves. One way to hang on to your inner life is by reading books.

The issue of obesity is very fashionable at the moment. Did you consciously write the novel with that in mind?

No, the story doesn't attempt to address the general issue of obesity. Mickey has his own very liberal views – he believes that he has a right to be as fat as he wants – but they're not necessarily mine. The novel was in fact written well before obesity became a matter of major public interest. I'd been writing a series of very tightly organized short stories, which had been an immense effort, and Mickey's story came as a piece of light relief. Once it was finished I didn't know what to make of it, and I shut it away in a drawer for about three years before I showed it to anyone at all. I think it's usually a good idea to shut novels away. Like wine – they either improve with age, or they go off.

When you say you didn't know what to make of it, what do you mean?

I was aware that it was a curiosity. The book trade likes to put books into categories – thrillers, romantic fiction and so on – and I wasn't at all sure how a surreal narrative about a vastly overweight American would be categorized. Nor was I sure how to place it in relation to my own writing – it was unlike anything I'd written before. In the end I took it out of the drawer, dusted it down and found that I still liked Mickey a great deal. Then I rewrote and rewrote, as I always do.

What will the next novel be like?

Different.